Safe at Second

Safe at Second

SCOTT JOHNSON

PHILOMEL BOOKS ✦ NEW YORK

Safe at Second could not have been written without the generous assistance of many people. Charles J. Oestrich, M.D., of Milford, Connecticut, gave me patient and meticulous guidance on the symptoms, care, and aftereffects of eye trauma. Mary Fox-Alter, computer coordinator for Pleasantville High School, helped me with the details of a school computer network. Glenn Jensen, physical education teacher and varsity basketball coach for Pleasantville High School, instructed me on the Byzantine rules of NCAA recruiting. Jeff Laurie gave me high and tight critiques to help me dig in at the plate. Thanks always to my agent, Richard Parks, for believing, and to Michael Green, my editor at Philomel, who knew Paulie when he saw him. Finally, love and amazement for my wife, Susan, for calming the *Sturm und Drang* of the little boys downstairs and, of course, the big boy upstairs.

Text copyright © 1999 by Scott Johnson. All rights reserved.
This book, or parts thereof, may not be reproduced in any form
without permission in writing from the publisher, Philomel Books,
a division of Penguin Putnam Books for Young Readers,
345 Hudson Street, New York, NY 10014.
Published simultaneously in Canada. Printed in the United States.
Book design by Tony Sahara and Patrick Collins. The text is set in Minion.

Library of Congress Cataloging-in-Publication Data
Johnson, Scott.   Safe at second / by Scott Johnson.   p.   cm.
Summary: Paulie Lockwood's best friend Todd Bannister is destined for
the major leagues until a line drive to the head causes him to lose an eye
and they both must find a new future for themselves. [1. Baseball—Fiction.
2. Best friends—Fiction 3. Friendship—Fiction 4. Visually handicapped—
Fiction. 5. Physically handicapped—Fiction. 6. High schools—Fiction.
7. Schools—Fiction.]   I. Title   ISBN 0-399-23365-2
10   9   8   7   6   5   4   3   2   1
First Impression

For my mother and father

Contents

Baseball is only one half skill . . .
the other half is something else.
Something bigger.

—GEORGE ABBOTT AND
DOUGLASS WALLOP
Damn Yankees

Part One
PERSONAL ASSISTANT

Chapter 1

I wasn't on second half a minute before I thought about stealing third. It's not like I smacked a double or anything to get there—I got hit by a pitch and the next guy up walked. But if you're like me, a guy who only plays in the seventh inning of games that don't matter much, you've got to do something to make Coach Benedict look up from his clipboard and notice you.

"Two outs, Paulie," Coach Z, the old guy who helped out the varsity when he could, yelled from the bench.

I nodded. It wasn't as if stealing third was going to mean anything. It was only a scrimmage against Hazelton High. By this time Coach Benedict had put all the scrubs in, which explained my presence out there.

But the Hazelton pitcher wasn't paying *any* kind of attention to me, really, so I took another few steps off the bag. With a big jump I could slide into third, and maybe the throw would sail past the third baseman, and I could pick myself up and romp on home. . . .

Coach Z went through the signs. Come on, I thought. Flash *steal*. But it was nothing but *swing away* for Tommy Ricco up at bat.

I was invisible out there, me, Paulie Roy Lockwood, dancing another step or two off the bag.

So I ran. As the pitcher came out of his stretch, I stuck my head down and tore for third. I felt my legs churning beneath me, and when I looked up, there was the base, a little farther than I counted on. . . .

I leaped, hands out, like Superman through the air—

Then a wall. I hit a wall, but it was really a mouthful of dust and a hard *thump* on the side of my head, and a second afterward, the sting where the third baseman's glove had swiped my face. I never heard the ump call me out. I didn't have to. Before I even opened my eyes I heard the pounding of feet running off the field and halfhearted applause from the Hazelton side of the stands.

For a moment I felt maybe I should just keep clawing, dig my way under third base and hide there. Before I could spit all the dirt out of my mouth, I heard the guys from our bench.

"Who was that? Lockwood?"

"Who else?"

"With two outs, he tries to steal—can you believe it?"

I climbed to my feet, my face full of infield dirt. When I spotted Todd tossing his spikes and glove into his duffel bag, he rolled his eyes and shook his head.

Before I could hurry over to him, Coach Benedict passed right in front of me. He probably wouldn't have even turned my way if I had kept quiet. Of course, I didn't.

"I thought I could make it, Coach."

He paused to look me up and down. I'm kind of scrawny, and not too tall, so it didn't take long. "Two outs, Lockwood, right?"

"Uh," I patted the dirt from my uniform, "right."

"Steal sign on?"

"Huh-uh. No."

He let me dangle a horrible second longer, then nodded and walked away. I was stuck there, still two feet from third, when I felt somebody grab my arm. Coach Z—the *Z* stood for Zimler—looked me straight in the eye. He was probably close to sixty, with a big round face, bulging cheeks, and tiny eyes. When he took off his hat you could see a bristle or two of hair. A lot of the guys made fun of Coach Z, but not me. Now that I was a junior and trying out for the varsity, it was good to have him around. Even though these were fall workouts, and the team roster wasn't supposed to be permanent until spring, I knew I needed a miracle to even earn the last spot on the bench. Coach Z didn't seem much like a miracle, but I was grateful to have him on my side.

"Coach," I said. "I cost us the game." I could see Todd waiting for me at the edge of the field.

Coach Z said, "Forget the game. Paulie, how're you ever going to steal if you don't pivot on your right foot?"

And for the next five minutes he had me shuffling around in the dirt, his hands on my shoulders, showing me how to get a jump on the pitcher. "Dig, pivot, *zoom*. Dig, pivot, *zoom*," he kept saying. It must have looked hilarious, if anyone but Todd had hung around to watch.

At last he let me go. "Now you know something," he said with his crinkly smile. I thanked him, gathered up my glove, and trotted over to Todd.

"Stealing third with two outs," Todd said. "Was *that* dumb."

"Thanks. Thanks a lot."

"Not just dumb," he said. "*Bonehead.*" I knew he was only having fun. Todd was about the best high school pitcher in the universe, so good there wasn't a week went by when he didn't get a phone call or letter from some pro scout or college coach. I couldn't remember him making a third out in his life; how was he supposed to know how I felt? "A bonehead play." Todd laughed. "That's what Benedict would say."

At Benedict's name I looked up suddenly. "Listen, you were sitting right near him. When I got thrown out, did he, like, say anything?"

Todd thought a second. We could see Melissa, Todd's girlfriend, leaning against her beat up old Dodge in the lot. "Nah. I don't think so."

"Well, maybe not *say* anything, but did he, like, have an *expression* on his face? Did he—"

"Paulie, I wasn't really watching—"

"Did he write anything down on his clipboard?"

"Oh, *yeah.*" Todd clapped a hand to his forehead. "I just remembered. I think he crossed a line through your name." But he couldn't keep down the grin.

"You're a bastard," I said.

"Paulie, lighten up. So you got thrown out. You're not going to make the team *or* get cut based on that."

"On what, then?" I heard my voice rise. "On what?"

"By the way," he suddenly mumbled without turning toward me, "I meant to tell you, Melissa's been kind of, uh, edgy, lately, so—"

"So if you guys start yelling at each other I should just let it go by, right?"

"Right." He smiled tightly, waving to her. "What a pal."

They went at each other immediately.

"Why are you late?" Melissa said, before Todd could even lean in to kiss her.

"Who said I'm late?"

"What am I, your chauffeur? Do you know how long I had to wait—"

"So who asked you to?" He snapped back. I ducked my head and looked for cover. "Anyway," Todd motioned his head toward me, smirking, "it was Paulie's fault."

Melissa took a quick peek over her shoulder. "Hi, Paulie." As usual I was an afterthought.

"Hey, listen, Melissa," I called. "I can walk."

"You're getting a ride." She got behind the wheel. "Get in."

When Melissa tossed back her dark brown hair and ordered me around like that, I knew better than to argue. She sure didn't look like a threat; her lips were full, and most of the time pursed, as if she were nursing some silent hurt. But her hazel eyes could go from dreamy to focused to fierce in under a second if you said something that pissed her off, even if you only meant it to be teasing. Which most of the time, I did. The last couple of months, hanging out with her and Todd was like having a ringside seat at Caesar's Palace. You'd think two people who had been going together as long as they had—almost two years now—could get their problems worked out, and I could have some peace.

"What is it this time?" Todd watched her through the passenger side door before getting in. "Just me, or—"

"No, it's not *just you*. Okay? Did you see *Panther Paws* today?"

Melissa was the editor-in-chief of the Edgeview school newspaper, and to hear her tell it, the only staff member who could read or write.

"I didn't," I said, trying to help out.

"*Of course* you didn't," she snarled. "That's because Maethner made us pull every copy out of every homeroom teacher's mailbox before anybody saw them." As if driving wasn't at all important anymore she turned completely around and handed me a copy. "Look at the front page."

I unrolled the paper and saw a photo of Mr. Manuel, the Spanish teacher. The headline read: *Edgeview Bids Adios to Much-Loved Teacher.*

"Too bad he's retiring," I said. "He's a nice guy."

"*Look at the photo*," Melissa screeched, slamming on the brake at a red light and jerking us all forward.

Todd leaned over so we both could see. The photo showed old Mr. Manuel with his shy smile standing at the front of his classroom.

"Look what's on the blackboard," Melissa said.

Todd and I read the letters together. "S . . . T . . . U"—we turned to each other—"D." It hit us at the same time. "*Stud.*" We exploded into laughter. "Mr. Manuel—*stud*," Todd snickered.

"It's supposed to be *study*," Melissa growled. "You know,

he always writes *study hard* on the board. But then he stood in front of the *Y*. And my *photographer* didn't notice it, and my *layout editor* didn't notice it—"

"And you didn't notice it," Todd finished for her.

"But *Maethner*," she sighed from the driver's seat, "Maethner noticed it. 'Melissa,' " she mocked the principal's deep bass voice, " 'You can't demean his dignity like that.' So now I've got eight hundred copies in my trunk and my car can't even make it over speed bumps. What about *my* dignity?"

Six seconds. That was how long Todd and I stifled ourselves before we erupted again, giggling like little kids.

"Appreciate the support, boys," Melissa said. "So," she glanced at Todd. "Are you coming over tonight?"

"Ah," he rubbed his brow, "I can't, I—"

"Okay, fine." Something had changed now, and we were a long way from laughing at Mr. Manuel.

"Melissa," Todd said. "It's just that there's this scout coming over tonight—"

"I said fine. Why should it bother me? Even though it's not like a scout's anything you ever cared about—"

"Who says I don't care?"

"You don't," she shrugged. "Why should you? You have these guys coming over all the time."

"Melissa, this is my future—"

"And you're so nonchalant about it. 'Sorry, Melissa.' And then you *smile*. Like you couldn't care less, about me or the scout. You know what I am? I'm just another appointment in your calendar. *Melissa Donovan, Friday, eight o'clock.*"

"Uh," Todd waited as long as he could, "by the way, about Friday. . . ."

"What, *another* scout?"

"No, a coach. From Mississippi State. It's a good baseball school." He grinned uneasily, and I cringed.

Melissa snapped. "It's so damn easy for you, isn't it? Being the big star."

"Well," I joined in, though if I were smart I would have been huddling in the trunk with all those copies of *Panther Paws*, "Todd really does put in a lot of work—"

"No, Paulie, she's right," Todd interrupted, now just as angry as she. "It is easy. I admit it. Okay, Melissa? But why should you get so upset. . . ."

It went on like that, all the way to Todd's house. I slumped down and shut up. When Melissa pulled up to the curb, they were still arguing. I tried to slip out my door.

"Paulie," Melissa caught me. "I said I'd drive you home."

"That's okay," I thought I'd try again, "it's only a couple of blocks." But right away she was back to wrangling with Todd. If I were lucky I could still make my getaway and—

"*Lockwood.*" All three of us winced at the whiny voice. "*Lockwood.*"

There, across the street, cupping his hands around his mouth, stood Chuckie Miles. I waved halfheartedly and tried to ease away, but I knew what was coming.

"Juan Gonzalez," he shouted, "1997."

Chuckie, not now, I motioned.

He repeated, "*1997.*" A plump junior with big glasses, he

shuffled to our side of the street. "I knew I'd stump you," he smirked.

I sighed. "He hit .296," I said wearily, "with forty-two homers."

Melissa stared at me as if I had just landed from Mars.

"Damn." Chuckie reeled backward in disappointment. "*Damn.*" He started to retrace his steps across the street when suddenly Todd called him over.

Melissa kept her eyes on me. "What was that all about?"

I watched Todd reach into his wallet, pull out a few bills, and pass them to Chuckie. With a smug grin Chuckie palmed the money, tugged loose a wrinkled wad of paper from his backpack, and handed it to Todd.

Before I could ask what he was doing, Todd turned to Melissa and answered for me. "Paulie knows every big league batting average for the last seven years."

"Earned run average, too," I threw in. Chuckie Miles was already halfway down the block. I looked curiously at Todd.

He ignored me and continued to Melissa. "It's Paulie's claim to fame."

Melissa looked puzzled. "Why," she asked, "would you know something like *that?*"

"It's from this stupid game he's got," Todd began, and his tone reminded Melissa they weren't through fighting.

"Don't call Paulie stupid," she barked at him.

"No," I defended Todd, "he means the game is stupid—"

"*What game?*" She turned back to me.

"Tabletop Pro Ball," Todd teased. "Tell her about it, Paulie."

"It's . . . it's just a game," I said weakly. "It's got dice, and a card for every big league player . . . with his stats. . . ." My voice trailed off.

"Paulie's been playing it since he was nine," Todd said. "What do you think gets Paulie through the winter when there's a foot of snow on the infield?" He winked at me. "Greg Maddux, 1995."

"Nineteen and two, 1.63 ERA."

Melissa slowly shook her head. "Get a life, Paulie."

"I don't have to," I said, reaching down for my duffel bag. "I've got baseball."

After Melissa drove off, Todd mumbled, "Sorry about the, uh, little tiff there. . . ."

"I don't see why you can't stop arguing."

"And what? Just get along?"

"Well, yeah."

"You make it sound so easy. Just wait till you get a girlfriend. And wait till you're seniors, and you don't know if you're going off to separate colleges, or whether one of you is going off to some rookie league in Florida, and whether you should stay together, or even if you *can* stay together—"

"Okay." I tried to wave him off. "Okay."

"—and maybe she's the one person in the world you figure you should be able to sit down with and talk to about a goddamn decision that's probably more important than you'll ever make again in your life, but every time you try you get into some stupid argument over who didn't return whose phone call, or—"

I was going to ask what was the deal with Chuckie Miles when my eyes fell on the green Cadillac with Missouri plates parked in front of his house. "Hey," I asked, "aren't you meeting some scout tonight?"

"Yeah," he nodded, looking past me at the car. "He's probably there now." He smiled. "You want to meet him?"

"What?"

"Didn't you ever want to meet one of these guys? See what they're like?"

"Sure." I laughed uneasily. "I guess so."

"Well," he clapped me on the back. "Follow me."

Todd didn't have any brothers or sisters, and his parents must have had him late. They always seemed a little more like grandparents to me, glad to settle in one spot and talk your arm off. My dad was the total opposite, always in a hurry. Even when you were in the middle of saying something he was halfway into the next room. But old or not, the Bannisters were about as nice as anybody I'd ever met. Every time I walked in their door I had the feeling they were preparing a surprise party just for me.

In the living room Mr. Bannister sat on the sofa next to a big guy in a gray sports jacket.

"Todd," Mr. Bannister said, just the trace of a scolding in his voice. "You remember Mr. Raycraft was going to join us for dinner tonight."

"Hello," Todd said. "Pleased to meet you." He had a deep, strong voice, and the way he confidently strode across the room and reached out his hand for Raycraft to shake was going to make up, I knew, for a lot of late appointments in his life. That and his fastball, of course.

"Mr. Raycraft," his dad said, as if to jog Todd's memory, "from the Cardinals."

"Right." Todd chatted with Raycraft for a minute or so about today's practice, how good the team looked for the spring, whether we'd make it back to the state finals. In that time Mrs. Bannister made at least two circuits from the kitchen, placing a tray of cheese puffs on the coffee table, clearing some glasses away. Finally Todd said, "Be with you in just a minute, Mr. Raycraft. I promised Paulie some chemistry notes."

"You take your time, Todd." Raycraft had large hands and thick, blunt fingers. I wondered if he had been a catcher once, and whether he had ever made it to the majors.

"They're in my room," Todd called to me, but I was in a trance, just picturing Raycraft in meetings with real pro ballplayers. I turned to Todd, startled. "The notes," he explained.

"Oh," I said, and followed him up.

Todd's room was what I imagined the Baseball Hall of Fame in Cooperstown was like. He had won so many trophies by now that the early ones, from Little League, were already in a box in his closet, and the recent ones—MVP, County Level I for the last two years, Pitcher of the Year for the last three, a gleaming loving cup from the state for High School Athlete of the Year, the balls mounted on pedestals from his seven no-hitters—were getting crowded together on the shelf, and it was a big shelf. The walls were covered with certificates, framed newspaper articles, and plaques.

"What chem notes?" I asked, thumbing through the fat envelopes from colleges that littered his desk.

"Here." He dug in his bag, and I saw the crumpled sheets he'd bought from Chuckie Miles. "Take them."

I felt my nose wrinkle, as if scenting something foul. "I was wondering what those were."

"They're chem notes. For your test tomorrow." When I didn't react, he said, "You've *got* a test tomorrow, don't you?"

"Of course I do." All week I had been raving about it to Todd as if it were some obnoxious cousin coming to visit. I did my best in chemistry—well, I tried—well, *sometimes* I tried, just like in all my other classes. But any enthusiasm I worked up for school never lasted long.

"So, now," Todd encouraged me, "you've got something to study."

"You *bought* those? For me? This is one of my dad's little tricks, isn't it?"

"I wish it was," Todd said. "Maybe *he* would have paid Chuckie Miles."

"I'm not studying those," I said evenly. "It wouldn't be right."

"Wouldn't be *right?*" Todd groaned. "They're not the *answers*, Paulie, they're just notes. Maybe if you study them—"

"Well, I'm not. I've got my pride."

"Wait—your pride won't let you look at these, but failing the test, that's okay."

"I won't fail. I'll get a C." I paused. He sprawled on the bed and watched me. "Or maybe a C minus."

"So what's wrong with getting a B? Or an A?"

"Maybe I will."

"Without studying?" Todd tried to sound indignant. "And here I go out of my way to get you—"

"*All right.*" I snatched the notes out of his hand. "Listen, I'm going to pay you back for this."

"Forget about it." Todd grinned, knowing he had won this one. "Besides, it doesn't hurt for that guy downstairs to think I'm a scholar or something, you know? Helping other kids? Maybe he'll offer more if he thinks he'll lose me to some college."

For the first time in a couple of minutes I thought about the scout. "Your mom and dad must really want you to sign with him. Your dad must have asked twelve times if he wanted something to drink."

Todd grimaced. "They're like that with every scout. And every college recruiter. Should I sign with the pros or go to college? They don't know *what* they want me to do. They get impressed by all those names. The University of Texas. The Toronto Blue Jays. Each one sounds better than the last."

He punched up his pillows behind him. "And then every so often Dad feels like he should help me decide. 'It's like this,' he says to me. 'It's like buying a Chevy or a Ford. With a Chevy you get this, and with a Ford you get that.' " Todd shook his head. "My dad's a great guy, you know, but sometimes he's absolutely clueless. He's talking Chevys and Fords, and I'm thinking what color my first Porsche should be."

We both started giggling, like thieves counting up the take. "Hey," I realized. "Shouldn't you get down there? Isn't that guy waiting for you?"

"Of course he's waiting for me. Paulie, that's the point."

16

Chapter 2

Todd was always looking out for me. When he wasn't getting me Chuckie Miles's chem notes he was helping me shovel snow off somebody's driveway so that I could make a few bucks to buy the new edition of Tabletop cards, and before that he was warning me whose yard I should never cut through because some Doberman was lurking there.

Maybe that was what friends did, they looked out for each other. It probably seemed to some people—sometimes I thought it, too—that mostly it was Todd looking out for me. But we knew better. I could take care of myself. That was probably how we got to be friends, back when we were on the same Little League team. I was in fifth grade and Todd was in sixth. Because I was kind of scrawny, because I went diving all over the field after balls I had no chance of catching, some of the older guys marked me for an easy target. It was just good old fun, I kept telling myself, when one yelled, "Think fast," and fired a ball at me from five feet away. Just fun, when another tripped me during sprints.

I stopped pretending it was fun during one of our first team scrimmages. I was standing at second, waiting for a throw from the outfield. Big Bobby Digget was trying to leg out a double. Maybe it was my fault. I might have been standing too close to the bag. But when he got into second, way ahead of the throw, he pulled up short, crossed his arms, and gave me a whack like an offensive tackle, knocking me to the muddy ground. When I looked back, Bobby wasn't even sorry. "Hey, dork," he taunted me. "Stay out of the way."

Nobody thought much of it. Guys were slipping all over the field that day. But I remembered. Two innings later Bobby Digget was on first. When the next batter grounded to short I covered second to take the throw. I could hear Bobby's feet make sucking sounds in the mud as he plodded toward me. When the shortstop flipped me the ball, I tagged the bag, and instead of stepping out of the way, I planted my feet, bent my knees, threw out my hip, and sent Bobby flying.

For one instant he was totally in the air, like an astronaut in zero gravity, and then *splat!* He landed sidelong in the mud. That was the third out, and I hurried off the field while Bobby slipped a few more times climbing to his feet. Everybody was laughing, of course, calling him the Mud Monster. Everybody but Todd. He caught my eye and winked. "Nice going," he said. It might have been the first thing he ever said to me.

The next inning, when Bobby came up again, Todd was pitching for our side, and drilled him with a fastball right in the butt. Bobby howled and clutched his rear end like a kid who'd just been spanked. When it was clear he was okay, the guys started teasing him all over again. I ignored it, and went up to Todd on the mound. I knew he had hit Bobby on purpose; that was the first pitch I'd ever seen him throw that wasn't a strike.

"I can take care of myself," I warned him. "Did you do that on my account?"

"Nah." He shook his head, sized me up, and grinned. "I did it 'cause that guy's a jerk."

We walked home together that day—it turned out we didn't live more than a few blocks away from each other—and we've really never been apart since. We must have been a funny sight—Todd tall and lean and a laid-back kind of strong, as if there was no end of energy he could call on when he needed it, and me—skinny and jittery, my reddish brown hair sticking out in odd tufts that I never could tame. Along the way I kept talking about big league pitchers, twenty-game winners, All-stars. And then I mentioned names he hadn't heard before: Bob Gibson, Bob Feller, Walter Johnson, and by his third puzzled "Who?" I halted him in the middle of the sidewalk.

"You don't know *anything* about baseball," I accused, "do you?"

For a second his face hardened. He wasn't used to people taking that tone with him.

"You know how to *pitch*," I said. "But you don't know anything about the game. The old guys. The Hall of Famers."

"Maybe I don't." He tried to laugh it off. "So who does?"

"I do," I exploded—I can get a little crazy when I'm all revved up on baseball—and for the rest of the way home he couldn't stop me. I raved about Gibson throwing so hard he always fell off the mound, and Walter Johnson's long, drawn-out windup. I made it sound as if I had been there, watching

Dizzy Dean and Satchel Paige, though of course I'd only seen them on faded videos and jerky film clips. But I'd seen them a million times in my head. *Nobody* knew more about baseball than I did. By the time we got to his house, I had made him feel like a little kid on his first trip to the museum.

We stood by his front steps. "Damn," he said. "I never heard of half of those guys."

"Well, you'd better learn." And I let the next thing drop, nonchalantly, just so he'd know I hadn't overlooked it. " 'Cause you're going to be right up there with them."

How did I know, that long ago? Hey, how could anybody miss it? Todd had Hall of Fame tattooed on his forehead. Back in sixth grade he already did all those things major leaguers did, and I don't just mean strike out two-thirds of the guys who faced him. To me, the little signs told it all: The way he'd stare through a batter, or take his time rubbing up a new ball till he had it just to his liking, no matter how long we had to wait. People never noticed those details; but then not everyone knew baseball like I did.

It wasn't just a game to me, I had meant what I said to Melissa—it was my life. I loved everything about it, even infield practice, where every ground ball was a new adventure. I didn't have much talent, I guess, I just liked that feeling, that a game would never end, that there was no clock ticking away. Sure, there were innings, but an inning could last forever if nobody made the third out, and there were no buzzers or two-minute warnings to send you home. When I wasn't playing Little League or bouncing the ball off the garage or throwing the dice for my Tabletop game, I was still thinking about baseball: Not winning or losing, or even making a dazzling play—just me, perched out there at second, pounding my glove and waiting for the next pitch.

Even after we got close, Todd never did learn the game the way I did. I scolded him for it. "You don't even *like* baseball— you just like being good at it." But all the time I knew that was what he liked me for, that was what made me special to him. There was no shortage of people telling him how great he was. But there was nobody like me, telling him how much he *didn't* know.

Because Melissa was right, of course. It did all come easy for Todd. As if his fastball weren't enough, once he learned he could snap off a curve it seemed to get easier still. You weren't supposed to throw curves in Little League, but by the fifth inning the other side was usually just watching Todd with their mouths hanging open. By then it didn't matter if he mixed in a killer curve once in a while; nobody complained. I learned pretty early, watching Todd, that there were lots of ways around the rules if you were good enough.

By the time Todd was in eighth grade everybody knew he was on some other level. A lot of the kids, even some adults, just started acting differently around him—tongue-tied, nervous. I'm not sure how it started. Maybe when somebody pointed out the local college coach in the stands, never taking his eyes off Todd. Maybe when the high school petitioned the county athletic board to allow Todd to play for the varsity, though he didn't even go to the high school yet (they said no). Maybe the way the stands were filling up more and more with strangers—

reporters, recruiters, even pro scouts. Pro scouts, we all whispered, for an eighth grader!

Edgeview, our town, was twenty miles north of Albany. Adults called it "peaceful," but even they said it with a grin, as if, like most of the kids, they were secretly wishing something would happen. That something was Todd. While I sweated through two years of junior varsity, he went right to the varsity team his freshman year. You could almost see Coach Benedict drooling in anticipation. Edgeview hadn't had a team above .500 in eight years. Now, with Todd, the whole town was talking county sectionals. By June, *Sports Illustrated* featured Todd in its "Faces in the Crowd" section. How good did a fifteen-year-old have to be to make it there? Try three consecutive no-hitters. Just three? Yeah, and the last one wasn't even a perfect game—the shortstop made an error.

In Todd's sophomore year *SI* did a full-length story on him. He had won thirty-two games in a row by then. One of the photos took up two pages. It showed Todd in the middle of his windup, the big number twenty-seven spread across his back, his right arm drawn back like a snake about to strike, his left leg up high. In another photo, of Todd leaning casually against his locker, the caption called him: "Edgeview's matinee star mound ace." When I asked what a matinee star was he said, "It means I'm good looking." And he was, I guess. By sophomore year he had shot up to six three. He had thick black hair that he always kept carefully trimmed, dark brown eyes, and a strong jaw that always looked as if he had his mind made up.

After the *SI* article came out, I could see a cocky streak in him. Todd had always been confident, but more and more he'd glare at an ump when he didn't get a call. Or during a game, if he thought a batter was digging in on him, he'd challenge him. "Hey, there's a fastball coming. Low and outside. Think you can hit it?"

He started hanging out with the seniors more. That was before Melissa, and it seemed he was going out with a different girl every weekend. Sometimes they took him to parties where I knew there was a lot of drinking. When I nagged him about that afterward, he only said, "You ought to come to one, Paulie."

"Right. A freshman at a senior party. They'd hang me from the ceiling. They'd make me into a *piñata*."

"No, they wouldn't," he said. "Not with me there."

Same old Todd, I told myself. Trying his best to look out for Paulie. And in high school, he had more reason to. It was turning out to be pretty tough for me. If I scraped and clawed I could maybe get B minuses, but mostly I got C's. Meanwhile Todd was strutting around as if he owned the school.

I could see why. There weren't too many things that didn't turn out his way. That spring we were in the same health class. It was just a few weeks after the *SI* article. Coach Benedict, who taught phys ed, was filling in for Mrs. Moscowitz. She left some lesson plans, but after five minutes Coach got bored and starting writing scrambled words like NIGHYEE on the board. The first person who called out "hygiene" was supposed to get extra credit. Todd never got involved with stuff like that; he just slumped back in his seat and watched. Near the end of the period the coach had drifted down our aisle and was standing right over Todd, when he made the mistake of looking down.

"Hey," the coach chided, and before anybody knew it he

had fished a pack of Marlboros out of Todd's pocket. "You know the rules. No smoking. Okay?"

"Okay," Todd nodded, still leaning back in his seat. "Can I have those back now?"

"Back?" Benedict chuckled. "I've got to hand it to you, Bannister." He returned to the front of the room with the cigarettes and sat on the edge of the desk. "Most guys would be saying, 'Coach, they're not mine, I swear, I'm holding them for a friend.'"

"No," Todd said. I could tell by his tone he didn't think this was funny. "They're mine. I'd like them back."

Coach shook his head. The rest of us sat up in our seats. "Well, too bad," he said. He leafed through some papers on the desk. "Now, let's see what kind of homework Mrs. Moscowitz has for you. . . ."

"I'd like them back," Todd said firmly, "or I quit."

We all heard it; Coach had to answer. "Quit what?"

Nobody breathed, but about a dozen heads turned to look at Todd.

"I'll quit the team," he said.

"You'd quit," Coach's voice sputtered; I could sense the other kids in the room, like me, wanting to squirm. "You'd quit over a pack of cigarettes?" He paused, as if adding up all his options, and then he chose the absolutely worst one. He folded his arms and said, "I don't believe you."

"All right," Todd said. "I quit."

I wanted to scream at him, *Are you crazy?* but I could barely swallow.

Coach looked pale. "What are you talking about, you quit?"

24

Todd said, "I'll bring in my uniform tomorrow."

Fifteen seconds passed like ten years, and then, luckily for the coach, the bell rang. Lucky because, as kids got up and headed for the door, he could flip Todd the pack of Marlboros, muttering, "Don't let me see those again," and maybe tell himself that nobody noticed. I sure did. Todd slipped the pack into his pocket. Out in the hall I shook my head. "That was a hell of a chance you took, making a threat like that."

"It wasn't a threat," he said.

"You were really going to quit over a stupid pack of cigarettes?"

"It wasn't the cigarettes, Paulie. It was Benedict."

"What if he stuck to it? What if he kicked you off the team?"

"He wouldn't have."

"But how do you *know?*" I said.

Todd looked at me. For a moment he seemed so icy and superior I could see why Benedict might have had it in for him. Right then I wasn't even sure I liked him all that much. "You know all those scouts, and all those reporters, and all those college recruiters who come to every game?"

"Yeah."

"What do you think?" He smiled. "They come to watch Benedict *coach?*"

Benedict never forgave him. He still pitched Todd as much as he could. He wanted to win, after all. But you could tell he didn't like him by the way he glowered at Todd when his back was turned, or how he was never first to congratulate him after a win.

Maybe that was why, when Todd did quit smoking, it had nothing to do with Benedict. A week after that health class we were walking home from his varsity game—one of those ho-hum numbers where he pitched a two-hitter and struck out eleven—when two little kids approached. They were skinny and shy, probably in fifth grade, and ready to run off if we even looked at them too hard. They wanted to know, holding out copies of the *Sports Illustrated* article, if they could have Todd's autograph. Todd said sure, and signed along the bottom of one of his photos. The kids were so excited they could hardly stand still. Once they had his autograph they started asking questions, one after the other. Did he want to pitch in the majors? Who was his favorite player? I could tell Todd was having fun answering them. Finally they asked if they could shake his hand. He gave them each a firm grip, and they headed off with huge grins.

"Better get used to that." I laughed. "You're probably only going to sign a gazillion of those before you're through."

"Ehh." He waved me off and smiled.

"No, really," I said. "I'll end up paying twenty bucks for your autograph at a card show someday. You won't even recognize me."

He must have heard something in my voice, for he glanced over. For what seemed like the first time in weeks, that cocky half smile was gone. "Maybe you'll be there, Paulie. Did you ever think about that? Maybe you'll . . . be my agent, or something."

"Oh, right. You'd go broke in a month."

"I know." He reached into his duffel bag for his cigarettes. "You can be my personal assistant."

"What's that?" I waited while he lit one up.

"Well," he exhaled sharply, "I'm not exactly sure. But everybody's got one. You just hang around, take my calls, keep creeps away. And I pay you, say, ten percent." He paused. "Well, maybe five. What do you think?"

"Personal assistant." I liked the sound of it. I especially liked the way he said it. Not like the Todd I'd seen so much of lately, the one who acted big and haughty, as if that's what people expected of him. I saw the Todd who was my best friend.

Personal assistant. It wasn't even the money that appealed to me. I knew that five percent of whatever Todd was going to make was a fortune, but I didn't care about that. What I pictured was after some play-off game or World Series win, I'd flash my clubhouse pass and work my way to his locker. He'd see me and smile broadly, wave me over. I'd cut right through the crowd, slap him a high five and say, "Nice going, pal." And when all the questions were answered and the press and all the hangers-on were gone, I'd get him the hell out of there, safely home. I know friends don't have to keep accounts, but it was nice to know that after years of Todd looking out for me, I could do the same for him.

"Damn," Todd said suddenly, and ripped the cigarette from his lips.

"What's the matter?"

He motioned over my shoulder. "They're watching me."

At the far side of the playground the two kids huddled

under a big oak tree. When I turned their way they ducked out of sight.

"So?" I asked. "What's it matter?"

"It doesn't," he said. "It doesn't matter at all." But I noticed he threw the cigarette away.

And after that, I wasn't sure I ever saw him smoke another. It wasn't just the smoking that stopped, either. The mouthing off, the swagger, the seniors' parties. In no time those were gone as well. Melissa came along pretty soon after that, so maybe it was her doing. Or maybe he was just growing up. It couldn't have been because of those two kids. It couldn't. But when I teased him about his fifth-grade fan club he always got irritated. "I'm just taking better care of myself," he'd say. "That's all." How dumb was I to think he'd care about two nerdy fifth graders, spying on him from behind a tree?

But he didn't fool me. Ever since Little League, Todd had known he was a star. That was the first time he knew he was a hero.

Chapter 3

After sixth period I heard Rishi Patel, the right fielder, say, "The list is up." That was all I needed. I took off at a cautious trot, but inside the words were ringing, *The list is up.* When the crowds in the hall thinned out, I flew down the stairs, my hand barely touching the railing, through Freshman hall, and finally down more stairs to the gym.

There were rows and rows of lockers before you got to the coaches' office. For a moment I felt like a mouse in a maze, confused. When I came to a clear aisle I raced to the end, and there, across from the gym office, was the bulletin board.

Suddenly I heard my heart banging away.

On a yellow-lined sheet, thumbtacked to the board, *Varsity Baseball* was written in large letters. Underneath that were two columns penciled in Coach Benedict's bumpy scrawl. Over the first column were the words *Spring Roster.* I forced my eyes away. Instead, taking a deep breath, I faced the other column.

Cuts, it read at the top.

That was Coach Benedict, all right. First Team All-American Sensitive Guy Squad.

Stop stalling, I told myself. Find your name and get it over with.

I ran through the list quickly, but before I knew it, I was at the bottom. And there was no *Lockwood*. I glanced again at the top. Coach wasn't much for alphabetical order, I could see. The first name was Consalino, then Boehm, Schuler, then Harkness. Maybe I missed it, I thought. Better check again.

But the second time through, it still wasn't there.

Was I in the right column? Yes, *Cuts*. And I knew these guys, most of them weren't any better than I was. Of course it was the cuts. And Paulie Roy Lockwood wasn't on it.

Which could only mean . . .

I leaned against the bulletin board, trembling as if a marching band were parading through my body and the bass drum had lodged in my forehead. Stay calm, I kept thinking. I took one step to the left, centered myself in front of the column, and read the *Spring Roster* list.

I wasn't on that one, either.

Back to *Cuts* again, just in case I missed it. But no. My name wasn't there . . . it wasn't anywhere.

In the distance I heard the bell to start seventh period. For the first time I thought of the chemistry class I was missing. But it didn't help. I couldn't move. I couldn't do anything.

Then I heard a cough from the coaches' office, behind me. I turned, my fingers and toes numb, and saw Coach Benedict through the doorway, sitting at his desk.

No, I thought. You're not going to ask him. . . .

I answered, But I have to!

No you don't, and if you had any sense you'd—

I'll just ask him. That's all.

You don't want to know. Get it? Wouldn't you rather—

"Lockwood?"

I jumped. Coach Benedict was watching me, his brow wrinkled curiously.

"Uh, hi, Coach."

"Don't you have a class right now?"

"I do, but—" Now, at last, I managed to move one foot. And then the other. But then, before I knew it, the both of them betrayed me, and I was shuffling into Coach's office while the rest of me screamed to escape.

"Coach." I cleared my throat. "There's something I wanted to ask you. . . ."

His desktop was covered with spiral score books, newspapers, and Styrofoam coffee cups. Sitting behind it, he seemed a mass of coiled muscles, as if at any moment a line drive might go shooting past and he wanted to be ready.

"I, uh, I was checking the list." I motioned to it; he rested his chin on his hand, and he didn't say a word to help me out of this. "And—I was wondering—about my name. . . ."

"Your name?" His eyebrows rose. Even that seemed athletic.

"Uh-huh. You know." But he didn't.

"I'm—" Oh, the hell with it. "Coach, my name's not up there." I saw the framed photo of last year's team, the Eastern Regional champs, on the wall behind him. "I mean, I was wondering, fall workouts are almost over, and I just—"

"Well," he cleared a little space at his desk as if he were going to draw me a picture. "It's like this, Lockwood—you don't have much of an arm, you know."

"I know," I agreed, to head him off.

"And," he paused, "you don't hit real good."

"No." I shrugged uncomfortably. "Not *real* good."

"Your defense is okay, but—"

"And I'm fast, Coach, right? I've got good speed?"

"Yeah, you've got speed—"

"You always say, 'Speed wins games.'"

"You're reckless, Lockwood. Trying to steal third the other day. And how many times have I seen you get picked off?"

"A few," I had to admit.

"In *practice*. Lockwood, *nobody* gets picked off in practice. Imagine what that would have cost us in a game."

You never *put* me in a game, I wanted to say.

"Now if you want me to go through every little thing—"

"I don't. I just want to know why my name's not on the list."

"You want to know *what?*"

"It's not on *either* list. It's not under *Spring Roster* and it's not under *Cuts*. It's like I was never even there."

Our eyes met. My God, I thought. I was *snarling* at the coach.

"I mean," I said, as if I could soften what had just come out. "See . . ."

But Coach was poking furiously through some papers on the desk, moving scorepads and catalogs around until he came upon a pencil. I noticed how the vein in his neck was twitching slightly.

He gave me a five-second stare. "You say you're not on the list?"

I swallowed, but my voice still grated in my ears like the sound of two rocks rubbed together. "Huh-uh."

He brushed past me to the bulletin board. Waiting till I followed, he leaned over, scanned the lists, found *Cuts*, and at the bottom scribbled *Lockwood*.

By then he wasn't even angry anymore. "I don't know what happened," he said. "I must have overlooked you." He pointed to my name. "All clear now?"

The whole business of cutting me from the team wasn't any more a nuisance than correcting an error in his grade book.

"Yeah," I said, and turned away. "I just wanted to be sure."

Maybe he didn't stay angry, but I sure did. It wasn't that I didn't make the team. No, *that* I didn't hold against him. But that I had to sit there and listen to every single detail why I stunk, as if I were a defective toaster some guy brought back to the courtesy desk—

But I couldn't keep it up. And by the time school ended I was only left with this: I didn't make it.

I didn't make it. I got cut. I wasn't good enough.

However I said it, it hurt just the same.

It was the first time in three weeks I had nowhere to go after school but straight home. I thought about heading to the field, where for another week or so the team would be going through the last few drills and scrimmages. Todd might be pitching. I could drop by the backstop and say hi. Even show Benedict, See? No hard feelings.

I'd do that the next day, definitely. Or Friday, for sure.

When I got home my mom and dad were huddled over the downstairs computer with my little brother, Tyler. They were tapping at keys and talking that weird computer language they got into sometimes: "Can I free up some more RAM?"—"No, no, right click"—"You're going to have to reconfigure for that"—"*right* click, I said, *right. . . .*"

Tyler was only a freshman, but he was already a computer fanatic, while I hardly even knew how to turn one on. My mom worked for an educational software company, and my dad—well, to tell the truth, I didn't really know what my dad did. I knew he was a "human resources consultant," but whenever he talked about work he never mentioned any humans—just computers.

"Practice over already?" Dad asked. He was wearing his spandex and his cross-trainers. I knew any second he'd be leaving for his run.

"Yeah. I, uh . . ." I thought about telling them, but held off. "It's over," I just said.

"Time on your hands," Dad kidded. "You're a lucky man." He set his Pacemaster watch till it was beeping the way he liked it and left by the back door.

"That's me," I said, but I knew he hadn't heard me. I lingered in the kitchen and thought about telling my mom, but she was already working the microwave control panel. Besides, I didn't so much want to tell her—I just wanted her to know. But with my mom there were no shortcuts. She was pretty slender (I guess I got my Incredible Hulk build from her), with a tiny mouth and a delicate chin, but the sharpest brown eyes that sized you up from behind her glasses. Whenever you said something to her she always waited a second or so before she answered. It was probably just a habit, but it always seemed as if she were thinking over whatever you said, and the problem was, it made you think it over, too. And because she didn't answer right away, it made you say more. Maybe more than you wanted to. Sometimes I wished she'd just jump on the end of whatever I was saying and finish it for me.

I ended up just heading to my room, where I cleared a pile of *Sports Illustrated*s off my bed and sprawled out. I didn't even reach for the light switch.

I took in all the pennants and posters and magazine photos I had cut out and tacked up on the walls when I was little, the dresser piled high with baseball cards, the old gloves in the corner. For a moment my vision got blurry; my God, I was ready to *cry*. I wiped a hand across my eyes. How crummy could it get, I thought. That you could love something more than anything in the world and still you couldn't have it.

The door swung open slowly. Tyler drifted in, his eyes behind his big glasses fixed on some computer printouts in front of him. He had the same build as I did—pretty skinny, in other words—but he always dressed as if he were already middle-aged, in button-down shirts and pressed khaki pants, never jeans.

"Paulie, listen to this." Suddenly he looked up. "Hey, why don't you turn on a light?"

"I like the dark." The last thing I wanted was a good clear look at myself in the mirror.

Tyler flicked on the lamp next to my bed, and sat on the

edge. "I was working over some figures, and look what I've got here."

Once I had to listen to him tell me the whole story of how some teacher had let her password expire in the school computer system, how Tyler found out and made up a new one for himself to use, and now he could zip around through all the school files. I started to protest, when he said, "No, listen, this is about Todd."

"I don't—what about Todd?"

"You were saying how he didn't know whether he should sign with the pros or go to college?"

"So?"

"So I worked out a little spreadsheet here." He ran a finger down a column. "Let's say he goes pro, and he goes to the majors right away. The first year he makes $150,000. That's major-league minimum. Then, in, let's say, three or four years, he's up to two, three million dollars a year—"

The numbers whizzed past me. "Tyler—"

"And then, when he goes free agent, let's say he signs for nine million a year, averaged over five years . . . and let's say he pitches for fifteen years in the majors. . . ."

"Wait a minute."

"So if he invests, say, one-tenth of what he makes, after taxes, at, say, six percent interest, over fifteen years, and if he rolls all that over and reinvests it—"

"But—"

"Wait, wait," Tyler signaled. He went on to price the cost of a college scholarship, and show me what Todd would lose in pro salary during those four years of school, not to mention what he would miss in endorsements. . . .

I leaped off the bed and fumbled for my jacket.

Tyler looked up. "I'm not done yet."

"That's okay." I stepped around him, through the doorway. "I'm not interested."

"What are you *talking* about," Tyler whined. "You were the one who asked me to *do* all this."

I lingered on the stairway. "I was?"

"Yeah. You said you needed to find out all this for Todd. You were going to be his . . . his . . ."

"Personal assistant," I said quietly.

"That's it." He followed me to the top of the stairs. "Hey, how come you came home early today?"

I searched his face hard, but he was just curious.

"No reason," I said. "I just did."

"So where are you going now?"

"To see Todd."

"Well, great." He looked enthused again. "Why don't you give him this?" He held out the printout.

"That's all right," I said. "I don't want to bother him. He's got a lot on his mind."

On the way to Todd's house I tried not to think about anything. Not the scene in Benedict's office. Not Tyler with Todd's future in his hands. As if my brain were a blackboard, I stood on guard, eraser in hand. But the brain just wouldn't give up, and when I started thinking about the High School Carnival two years ago, a part of me said, Aw, what's the harm in that, and I let the memories come.

It was back when I was a freshman. Some genius on the Fundraiser Committee thought up a Dunk-the-Clown booth, and the class officers seized on it.

All they needed was the clown. Of course it had to be a freshman. The kind of nerdy, overeager freshman who showed up a half hour early every day for spring tryouts, who always ran an extra lap without being asked to, and finally must have been noticed by some student government kids, watching practice from the stands.

I could have said no, I suppose. But when a couple of seniors cornered me and half flattered, half threatened that the whole carnival would collapse if Paulie Roy Lockwood and Paulie Roy Lockwood *only* weren't out there taking his dunks for the student body . . .

It wasn't really fun, but still I kind of enjoyed it. I sat up on a platform inside a wire cage, suspended over a barrel of water. You paid a dollar and got three throws. If you hit the target, a lever connected to the platform, I'd fall in. My part was to taunt the crowd so they'd be provoked to spend money on a chance to shut me up. In no time I realized there weren't that many people who could hit a bulls-eye from twenty-five feet away, and it made me cocky. I got into ranking on people strolling by. It helped that I wasn't particularly crazy about wearing a big red ball on my nose, a Bozo wig, and a striped jumpsuit with size twenty-two shoes, and as the day wore on I grew even nastier.

Then, in the late afternoon, I spied Todd and Melissa. They

had just started going out, and as they ambled past me I thought, Why not?

"Hey, superstar," I yelled. "Hey, loverboy."

Todd's head spun my way as he placed my voice.

"Yeah, you. You with the hot babe. Hey, Mr. *Sports Illustrated*, think you can throw a strike in the big time?"

He might have walked on if so many people hadn't turned his way.

"Nah, nah"—the great thing about being a clown, I realized, was that there was hardly *anything* you couldn't say—"Come on, Mr. Number One Draft Pick."

Surrounded by a curious crowd, Todd just stared at me, his face changing like Dr. Jekyll's in one of those old movies. Suddenly he turned away, leaving Melissa there. It surprised me. I thought he'd at least fling a ball or two my way. After all, I had just meant to rile him, not chase him away—

Then he was back. He pressed a wad of red stubs on the ticket taker and held out his hands for some balls.

And some more.

And some more after that, so many that Melissa had to hold them, too. By now it seemed just about everybody at the fair had gathered around.

"Can't hit me," I screeched. "Nah, nah." But I didn't sound so certain anymore.

Even to show me up Todd wasn't going to risk his arm. The first pitch was a lob, really, a warm-up toss, but still it was right on target, with just enough *zing* to plunk me in the barrel of water. I gulped and hacked and clawed my way back up. It was the first time all day that anybody had dunked me. I heard the cheers of the crowd. Just as I settled myself on the platform it fell right out from under me, and I was back in the water, thrashing about. The third, fourth, and fifth times Todd only waited for me to get a leg up over the edge before he dunked me again. He didn't even give me time to yell at him. He only fired fastball after fastball, a dozen, fifteen in a row, and sank me every time.

Finally I clung to the side of the barrel, sodden tufts of the Bozo wig dangling in my face. My red nose was somewhere behind me, bobbing in the tank. I panted for breath. The crowd was buzzing merrily. There were probably a dozen more guys who wanted a shot now, but that was it for me. Quitting time.

Suddenly two hands reached down, grabbed me, and helped me out of the barrel. I kneeled, coughed some more, and looked up to see Todd staring down at me.

I staggered to my feet, my hands forming fists, my drenched costume sagging around me. "Thanks a lot," I sputtered. "Thanks for humiliating me."

He shook his head. "You humiliated yourself."

"What's the matter," I shouted at him, "couldn't you stand to see old *Paulie* in the spotlight for once?"

"No," he said, pulling off my wig and rubbing at my makeup with a rag. "No, I couldn't stand it."

"You just didn't like me getting a little attention."

"Not that kind of attention, no," he said. "Paulie, anybody can be a clown."

It took me a long time just to get over being mad and realize what he meant. And even then, I didn't entirely forgive him for that public dunking. But now, on the way to his house, I knew I needed him just as I had then, to pick me up. Even if he just sat there and listened. I'd say, quietly, *I didn't make the team,* and somehow I'd be all right. We'd hang out in his room just like always. He could show me something new that came in the mail that day, a follow-up letter from some pro scout, or another college with an even sweeter deal. . . .

I wasn't through the Bannisters' door more than fifteen seconds before Mrs. Bannister offered me dinner, then a snack, then something to drink, but I waved no thanks to all. "Todd's upstairs," she said. "I think Melissa's with him."

Okay, Melissa, no problem. I could tell her, too. Anyway, they were probably making out, and it wouldn't be the first time I walked in on them. They always yelled, *"Paulie, don't you ever knock?"* but I could tell they were never really mad.

I took the steps two at a time and burst into the room.

They sure weren't making out.

Todd was along one wall, and Melissa was sitting on his bed. They both jumped when I entered, but nobody spoke. I stared at their long, dark faces.

"I got cut," I said. Funny, when it finally came out, how easy it was to say. I nodded, and said it again. "From the team. I got cut. Benedict posted the list today."

There was an awkward pause, as if we were all waiting for me to get to the punch line of a joke I had forgotten how to tell.

"I just thought you guys would want to know."

Todd, at least, said something. "You got cut?" He sank into a chair, and sneaked a look at Melissa. "Jeez, Paulie. . . ."

Melissa, on the edge of his bed, tucked her legs up under

her. I looked closer. Her lashes were always black, and long, but now when she blinked—and she was blinking more and more as I watched—she left little dark smudges just below her eyes. She dabbed at them with her fingers, and then a tissue, but still they smeared. She gulped down a sob, but it didn't help to stop the tears. I turned back to Todd. He was staring down at his shoes. I could see him wince each time Melissa caught her breath.

"Hey," I said. "Don't worry. I just didn't make the team, that's all. It's not even important."

I knew whatever Melissa was crying about had nothing to do with me. So who was I reassuring? Me, I guess.

It's not even important.

Nice try, Paulie, I thought. You're no better a liar than you are a ballplayer.

Chapter 4

Maybe you only get one dream that comes true in your life. Maybe it's got to hurt enough, first. It's got to keep you lying awake all night, staring at the ceiling, until you realize you're crying for the first time in probably six or seven years. You wish morning would hurry up, as if morning would make things any better, but when you look over at the glowing red numbers of your bed stand clock it's still just three A.M., and that's the worst time of all to cry.

This is how my dream came true.

At phys ed the next day, I was slumping upstairs to the gym, passing the last of the lockers, the coaches' office—the bulletin board. And I gave in. I had to, the way you pick at a scab just to see how bad you were really hurt. All you're doing is opening up the wound underneath all over again, even making it worse. But I couldn't help it. I looked at the list, and instantly I knew something was different. Where Benedict had added my name there was now a large black cross out. I blinked and looked harder. It was *seriously* crossed out, as if nobody was supposed to know what was under the—

And now I was scanning the *Spring Roster* column, a roaring sound in my ears—

Bannister . . . Shawn . . . Patel . . .

My chest too tight for me to breathe—

Bates . . . Ricco . . .

Lockwood.

I squinted hard.

Lockwood.

I stretched out my fingers and touched the letters of my name as if they were written in Braille.

Lockwood. Like any other name up there. The last name on the list, but who cared? Maybe an extra varsity uniform, moth-eaten and musty, had turned up in the back of some locker, and rather than throw it out, Coach had thought of me.

Paulie Roy Lockwood, a member of the team.

I let out one fierce yelp of joy, and I could still hear the echo ringing off the lockers by the time I made it upstairs to the gym.

No way was I asking any questions. I wasn't even going near Benedict if I could help it. Why give him a chance to change his mind? Besides, he hardly looked my way all afternoon. I was the first one at practice, of course, and I was floating the whole time, even when Steve Bates, the starting second baseman, came over and stared at my muddy sweats. He was a beefy guy, dumb as a fire hydrant, who butchered so many ground balls he made me look like a Gold Glove fielder. But in the batter's box he was fierce; sometimes he took so mighty a swing both his feet rose up from the ground.

"Lockwood, I don't get it," he looked down at me. "You never play, but your sweats are always dirty." Tommy Ricco and

Ozzie Fuentes were standing nearby. Bates pointed to my nicked-up forearms. "Check it out," he called to them. "You ever see a guy get so banged up sitting on the bench?"

"What'd you do, Lockwood," Tommy Ricco laughed, "trip over the bats?"

I didn't say anything, just held my glove up to my face so they couldn't see I was still grinning, even through all their razzing.

Old Coach Z came puffing over to us in that bowlegged half trot. "If you want to know why he's so dirty," Coach Z scolded them, "you ought to look at what he does. Warms up the pitchers between innings. That right, Paulie?"

I nodded, looking down in embarrassment.

"Dives for those ground balls, right? Even in practice?"

I shrugged. "I guess. . . ."

"Sure you do." He faced the guys. "He's chasing down those foul balls, taking extra infield, coaching first—you big shots, you know, you might want to take a lesson or two from Paulie here. There's nothing out here he doesn't do."

"Except play," Ozzie mumbled, and the guys started snickering.

"Go on, get out there and shag some flies," Coach Z said. They groaned and moved off.

I was still beaming when Todd came in from running with the pitchers in the outfield. "Hey," he called, while he tossed the ball lightly to me, getting loose, "what happened? I thought you said you got cut."

"*Shhh.*" I glanced around. "I thought I was. Maybe Benedict just felt sorry for me. Or maybe he likes the way I hustle."

"Or maybe he needs somebody to keep score."

"Thanks."

"Hey, just kidding. Congrats, man. I mean it."

I was feeling so good the next thing I knew I was going through my own windup as I threw the ball back to Todd, kicking my leg a little, drawing my arm back, just as if I were a pitcher, too. One of my throws landed in the dirt and Todd had to chase it. When the next one bounced in he snapped, *"Paulie."*

I wound up and tossed another. For a while it wobbled and fluttered in the air, and then died about six feet in front of him. He frowned. I said, "I'm just practicing my—"

"I know, I know," Todd shook his head with contempt. "It's your knuckle curve."

"My *knurve*," I insisted. "My knurve."

"Okay, and you know what? It's *garbage*. It doesn't do anything but bounce in the dirt."

"What's the matter?" I grinned. "Jealous? Hey, you going to tell me what was going on with Melissa in your room yesterday?"

I was sorry I said it as soon as I saw his face.

"What I'm saying is," I tried to smooth it over, "am I going to have to sit through another fight in the car this afternoon?"

"Melissa's not picking us up today." Something in his voice made me stop, mid-throw.

"What's that mean?" I asked.

"That means . . . that means we broke up, Paulie."

"But . . . why?" I flipped him the ball. "What's the reason?"

"There's no reason. Or nothing's ever the *whole* reason. All

I know is we keep fighting every time we're together, and when we're not fighting we're talking about *why* we fight so much."

We tossed the ball in silence a few times. I had never seen him this way, his face fighting hard not to show a thing, looking all the more lonely for the effort. And here I was, his best friend, with no idea how to help him. I *wanted* to—I think I'd always been waiting for the chance to look out for Todd as he always did for me. I just never imagined it would happen like this. What could I say, so suddenly? I needed a little time to get ready. Then I'd help him. I knew I could.

Instead—boy, what a flop I was—I tried to brush it all away, saying loud and lighthearted, "Ahh, you guys'll work it out. You're crazy about each other."

Todd said, "I don't know if that's enough."

And while I groped for an answer, his first real fastball burned into my glove. I watched him pace himself, a full twenty seconds, before he threw again. This one stung. I wanted to say, Hold on, let me go borrow a catcher's glove, but there was no interrupting him now. I settled down in a crouch. Once I hollered, "Try a curve," just to say something, but he ignored me, working the strike zone methodically with his fastball: inside corner, belt high, outside corner, down around the knees. My left hand was nearly numb, and the pain had worked into my wrist. But when I looked up and saw his eyes so intent, I knew Melissa, at least, was a million miles from his thoughts. I crouched there, my glove hand stinging, and suffered in silence.

That night, my dad and I had a talk.

I always knew when they were coming. When he wanted

me to empty the garbage or mow the lawn he just hollered up the stairs. But for talks he always knocked lightly, peeked in the doorway, patting the back of his head as if he still couldn't believe he was getting a bald spot.

"Paulie, I was thinking," he said this time. "Maybe we should talk. . . ."

Talk about college, he meant. He couldn't fool me.

Dad sat on the bed. "I was thinking, once baseball practice is over, we might begin to think seriously about the SATs. This is your junior year—they're coming up, you know. Maybe we could get you some tutoring. . . ."

"Ah," I tried to wave it off, "that's okay."

He smiled at that, though he didn't look pleased. "Well," he said, already taking on that *tone* of his, "if you think you're just going to waltz into some SUNY school with mediocre college board scores. . . ."

I had to laugh. When I was little Dad used to talk about my going somewhere like Harvard or Amherst. By the time I was in middle school he had dropped that and started pushing SUNY, the New York state schools. But the truth was, I wasn't really sure I wanted to go to college. It wasn't as if I had anything better to do. I wasn't joining the army. I wasn't that eager to learn a trade. But college . . .

Whenever kids at school talked about college it was always who was going to make it to the Final Four, or how drunk somebody's older brother got one weekend, or how good-looking the women were, or how the cops had to break up some wild frat party.

48

They didn't know anything about college.

I did. It was seven or eight years ago, when my dad started taking courses down in Albany. He was changing jobs, working on a degree. None of that meant much to me back then. The only thing I remembered was before he took those classes it seemed he always had time to play some catch with me in the backyard. For the next couple of years it seemed all I saw of him was a rumpled-looking guy with a five o'clock shadow, tired from a full day of work, hunched over his textbooks and manuals and hacking away at a keyboard at the dining room table. A lot of nights he wasn't halfway through his work when I'd say good night, and there were a few times he hardly turned when I did.

That was around the time I started being close friends with Todd, so it didn't bother me that much. Dad changed jobs around then, and I guess he was a success. We got a new car, a bigger TV. He started wearing suits. Then he got a promotion, and the business cards he had ordered weren't good enough, so he got some newer ones. Once he had to give a presentation at a conference, and for two weeks straight he rehearsed it on Mom and Tyler and me. There were some parts where Mom would always laugh, and so would Tyler—but what was supposed to be funny I never did figure out. At the end I clapped for him just the same.

Dad and I never did get back to tossing the ball around after dinner. Tyler started grabbing Dad as soon as he walked in the door each evening, telling him about some *killer app* he had thought up, and Dad would get caught up in computer talk for a half hour. When he did get around to me it was never just to hang out, watch a game on TV, play some Tabletop. It was always for a *reason*—to help me with my homework, or have a *talk*. Nothing so aimless as tossing a baseball back and forth.

"Dad," I said. "I was just thinking . . . maybe I don't have to take the SATs. Maybe—"

"*Not take the SATs?*" Dad sat upright. "How are you getting to college without the SATs?"

"Well, uh . . . since you brought it up. . . ."

"*Paulie.*"

"Come on, Dad," I said. "Why do I have to go to college? I can hardly stand high school. My grades stink."

"They're C's. That's not so bad. And if you worked a little—"

"But what good is college, for me? There's nothing I want to do that college—"

"*That's what I mean,*" he shouted, then all at once grew calm. "What *do* you want to do, Paulie? That's why we're talking. What kind of career do you want?"

I squirmed. "I don't know. I—"

"Well, maybe you'd better start thinking about it. You don't have all the time in the world, you know."

"But Dad—why do you have to hit me with all this stuff now? This is a special day." I looked up at him. "I made the team today."

"You did? That's great." He cracked a wide grin and held out his hand.

I shook it, thinking yesterday I'm off the team, today I'm on it—either way Dad didn't have a clue.

50

◆ ◆ ◆

Before I went to bed I always played a game of Tabletop. Tabletop was great because, after it got too dark to play catch outside or all of your friends had gone home for dinner, or your dad could only take so much of your bouncing the ball off the garage door, Tabletop was always there, waiting.

Usually I managed both teams as if it were a case of life or death. I used to do the play-by-play, too, even announced the score at the end of each inning, just as if we were going to commercial. For a long time Tyler used to nag me to let him play. "You're too young," I held him off. Then by the time he was in fifth grade he was so deep into computers he couldn't care less about Tabletop.

Except at some point he must have realized how funny it could be if you had a brother who went upstairs every night, played a game by himself, and talked out loud all through it.

So he taped me.

The little creep taped me, secretly, one night, holding a microphone to the door of my room, and then he played it back for all his bratty fifth-grade friends about a million times. I couldn't go anywhere in town without some kid hardly into puberty yelling out, "Hey, Paulie, back, back, back, back—OUT OF HERE," the way I did when somebody homered in Tabletop.

I still loved Tabletop, though after that I didn't do the play-by-play out loud anymore. Tonight, though, I had trouble concentrating. Not from excitement—though I still should have been bouncing off the walls from news of making the team. Instead, I kept thinking how close I had come to being *off* the team. And then my dad's talk. And Todd and Melissa. And finally, just Todd. Wondering if some day, in ten years or so, I really would be Todd's personal assistant, or just a guy sitting here holding one of Todd's Tabletop cards in my hand, still doing the play-by-play (*"and Bannister blows the batter away with a high, hard one"*) when I hadn't even talked to him in years.

Just then I heard a creak from the hall, outside my room. I waited, and listened, and though I didn't hear it again, I didn't need convincing. Tyler—back for more.

I leaped from my desk to the door in one step, threw it open, and shouted, "Caught you!"

To the empty hall.

"Tyler," I yelled. "*Tyler.*"

The door to his room opened. He peered out, a paperback copy of *Great Expectations* in his hand. "What?"

"Were you listening to me play Tabletop? Were you taping me?"

"Why would I do that?"

"You did once."

"Yeah, when I was a little kid." He waved the book angrily at me. "Before I had *tests* on guys like *Charles Dickens.* What about you? Don't you have anything to do?"

"I had some homework," I stammered. "I got it done. Most of it."

"You're lucky," he said, "you're not in honors. You should be thankful."

I watched him go back into his room and close the door. "Yeah," I agreed. "I am."

Chapter 5

For the last scrimmage, against St. Hubert's, Coach Benedict had us wearing our uniforms. Todd was pitching, which would have been great, but the way he was mowing them down, the game would be over in no time. Any minute Coach would be saying: *Uniforms due on Monday, see you in the spring.*

Turn in my uniform? Already? I could hardly stop fingering it as I stood along the foul line. It wasn't new or anything, the waistband was all stretched out and it bagged in the seat, but compared to the JV uniforms . . .

"Paulie."

Even the way they stitched *Panthers* across the front . . .

"Paulie."

Coach Z was getting peeved with me. We were supposed to be working on my throws to first, and this was the third time he had caught me daydreaming. Once again he showed me in slow motion how to follow through with my whole body so my throws wouldn't sail off. "It's like this, see? You've got to bend your back."

"Yeah, Coach. I get it." I tossed him the ball.

"You didn't bend your back."

I sighed and tried again.

"Better," he frowned. "Now again."

I took a peek at Todd. By now he was unconscious out there, just firing fastball after fastball. In the stands I counted at least five scouts, older guys with paper coffee cups, clipboards, and stopwatches.

"Come on," Coach Z scolded me. "Get your mind in the game."

"But, Coach," I said, turning away from Todd, "I'm not *in* the—"

Out of the corner of my eye I saw it, and heard the two sounds almost together. The solid *ping* of a line drive off the bat. Then the ugly *clunk,* as the ball smacked into Todd's face and jerked his whole head backward.

From all around the field I heard one loud, sharp gasp.

I stampeded over with everyone else. Todd had landed hard on his right shoulder, and now, sprawling halfway off the mound, he looked as still and lumpy as an old duffel bag full of bats. Some of the guys on the field got to him first, and as I came up, one of them, Wayne Linder, turned away, his face white and sickly. I eased past him to get closer.

"Get back," somebody said. "Don't crowd him."

I saw from the slight rise of his chest that at least he was breathing. He must have been knocked out, and now was coming to. A couple of guys reached for his legs to try to straighten him out. Somebody else yelled, "Don't move him, don't move him."

"He's okay," I heard myself whisper, and kneeled down behind him to put my hand half around his left shoulder. "He's all right."

That was when he screamed. The ring of guys surrounding him fell back at the sound. I could feel him shaking under my touch as he dug his cleats into the dirt.

Coach Benedict stepped into the circle; guys automatically moved aside for him. You would have thought we were in second grade the way we all turned to him to make things right. He crouched down, checked Todd's pulse.

"He's all right," I murmured, but Todd howled again and wriggled his head and shoulders as if he could bury himself in the ground. "Just lie still," I tried to tell him.

"Line drive," someone muttered, and I spied the ball, a little way off the mound.

Todd shifted around and I saw his face.

The whole right side looked larger. The brow and cheek and part of his nose had begun to swell so much I couldn't even see the eye, just a trickle of blood, and dirt from the pitcher's mound caking the side of his face.

Todd, fully conscious now, tried to sit up, choked for a good breath, then let it all out in a shrill, panicky groan.

Guys were up on their feet, bumping into each other, nobody sure what to do. At the edge of the circle I saw the St. Hubert's kid who had hit the ball, wringing his hands, swallowing. Todd was twisting in pain now, as if he could tuck his face down into his belly and curl the rest of his body around it.

"Right in the eye," someone said, in a queasy voice.

And Benedict, still, hadn't done anything. It was the scariest thing, this big, muscular guy, kneeling at Todd's side, just as helpless as I was.

"Somebody call an ambulance," he said at last. "Austin, run over by the pavilion, there's a phone."

I heard Coach Z's wheezy tone. "Gene, we can get him to the emergency room faster ourselves."

"Yeah," Benedict said, rising, still keeping one hand on Todd. "Yeah. We'll take my car. Uh, Rishi, you help, and—"

"Me," I said. "Come on, Rishi." We tried to prop Todd upright. He was quivering all over now, as if he had the chills. I slipped his right arm over my shoulder. Todd was taller than I was, and the right side of his face fell against mine. I tried to lean away. Coach Z, who had fished some ice cubes out of the water cooler and wrapped them in a towel, pressed them up against the swelling. But with every step Todd winced, and we ended up just hurrying him to Benedict's car.

I don't remember much of the drive. Just that Benedict, still dazed, made a wrong turn or two, and Rishi, in the front seat, started giving him directions to the hospital, which Coach repeated in a spooky, numb voice. I tried to keep Todd steady in the back. Every time we speeded up he flinched at the motion, so I started cradling him against my chest. There were daubs of blood all over my shoulder. I tried to use the ice, and then I just gave up and wrapped my other arm around him. I could feel his breath on my face. Whenever he shuddered deeply I knew he was set to cry out in pain, so I tried to beat him to it. "It's going to be fine," I whispered in his ear. "You're going to be all right." Sometimes his breath would hiss out then, softly, and for a few seconds, until the next shiver of pain, I could almost believe it myself.

Chapter 6

They wouldn't let me in to see him till two days later.

I went as soon as school was over. At first I hesitated at the door to his room, peeking in. The TV was off, the lights were off, and Todd sat up in bed wearing huge sunglasses. He looked like one of those jazz musicians on the covers of my dad's old albums, his face, even in the dim light, pale. His hair was slicked back, and needed washing. The hospital nightshirt looked starchy. A long tube ran to his left arm from an IV bottle on a rack beside the bed.

His voice was a little higher than normal, and tired. "I still get headaches. They said I had a concussion. So they didn't know if I should have too many visitors. But the doctor, even the nurses"—he looked at me through the huge, dark lenses— "everybody's so damn *nice*. . . ."

"Are you going to be all right?"

"Oh, sure." He tried to prop himself up some more. "I mean," he mumbled for just a moment, "they don't know yet, really. They did an operation right away, trying to fix up . . ." He paused. "Where the retina got all torn up. Detached, they called it. Now they're just waiting. Every day the doctor comes in, looks me over." Todd shrugged.

"Waiting," I heard the scratchy sound of my voice, "for . . ."

"Hey, you know who was here this morning?" Todd grimaced for an instant, laying a hand on his right temple. "Benedict. Can you believe that? I always thought, you know, Benedict wouldn't give me the time of day if I wasn't the big star. But he was here, first thing. And after him, Coach Z."

Todd kept blowing his nose as he talked, wadding up the tissues and tossing them toward the wastebasket beside the bed. Sometimes he missed by a foot or so.

"And just before you, Melissa was here." In those oversize glasses he looked like some kind of wired, fast-talking ant. "Cut A.P. Calc, too, can you believe that?"

And then I knew what was wrong. He just didn't sound like Todd. Todd always took the little favors that everyone threw his way with a sly smile or a wink. I wasn't used to hearing him catalog all his visitors like some lonely kid counting up his friends.

"Well, that's great," I said. "Do you . . . do you remember anything about—"

"About getting hit?" He said it so easily, as if he were talking about something from long ago. "Not a thing. Just . . . I remember, going into the windup, and then . . . nothing. Just, a punch. Like I got punched in the face, but I don't remember. . . ." Todd's voice was quieter now. "I remember all this bouncing around. In a car. And—"

"That was me," I said. "I was holding on to you. In Benedict's car. That was me there."

He nodded. Now I could barely hear him. "And then, everything . . . really bright."

"The emergency room. I was there, too. Well, out in the waiting room."

"Yeah. And then"—Todd turned his head all the way around to look at me where I sat on his right side—"and then I woke up here." He gestured around at the dark room. "Here in Molesville." He laughed, and so did I. Suddenly he winced, and touched his brow above the glasses. "This is worse than a hangover." It wasn't that funny, but I snickered along with him.

A little after that his doctor came in, a middle-aged woman with her hair in a tight bun. She was nice, though, she even apologized for interrupting. "I just have to check a few things with Todd. It won't take long."

Right away Todd started backing up in the bed as if he'd discovered a tarantula down at the other end. "Well, hey," he said to me, "Paulie, thanks a lot for coming in. . . ."

"Oh, he doesn't have to leave." She turned on the overhead light and I blinked. "I just—"

"Ah, this is boring," Todd said. "Paulie, I'll call you tonight."

"I don't mind," I said. "I'll stay."

"Of course," the doctor said, "if Todd's tired, I'll have to ask you to leave."

I looked at him. It wasn't easy reading his feelings behind dark glasses, but something strange was going on. "Is that it?" I asked. "You tired?" He avoided answering for a moment, then shrugged no. "Then I want to stay," I said.

He sighed. "It's okay," he told the doctor.

For the next several minutes they acted as if I weren't even there. A good thing, too, for as soon as the doctor removed

Todd's sunglasses and I got my first glimpse of his right eye, I gasped.

There was a ring of puffy, tender red and white skin, and inside that a perfect circle of shiny black, as if he'd been smacked by a heavyweight champ. But the eye—the eye was a deep blood red. I had to hold my head down for a second so I wouldn't get sick. When I looked again I could spot where the pupil was, barely. It looked as if someone had plucked out his right eye and left a dark red stone in its place.

That was why he wanted me to go, I realized. So I wouldn't have to see how ugly it was. He was still looking out for me, even from his hospital bed.

I felt queasy, and then I shook that off and made myself watch. The doctor held a penlight a few inches from his pupil. "Do you see anything?" she asked.

"Nothing," Todd said.

She shifted the light a little, and asked again. "Nothing," he answered, and again, "nothing," and as she tried from all angles, the tone of his voice grew stronger, heartier. "Nope, nothing there," he said, as if he had posed the doctor a riddle and try as she might, she couldn't crack it. "Nothing," he said. His lips were tight, almost fixed in a grin. "Nothing."

A couple of evenings later I stopped by to see Todd's parents and drop off some assignments that Mr. Hedstrom, his guidance counselor, had collected from the teachers.

"Thanks, Paulie," Mr. Bannister said. "I know Todd'll appreciate this." But as I went through the assignments, I could tell he wasn't really listening. He still wore his white shirt from work, but it was all crumpled, and his hair was mussed. He ran his hands listlessly over the books. Well, what did I expect? He and Mrs. Bannister had been doing double shifts at the hospital for almost five days now.

"If you want I can bring these to him myself. I'm probably going over there, tomorrow."

"That's all right." Mrs. Bannister set out some coffee cake at the dining room table and we all sat down. "I'll be there early. Paulie . . ." She took a breath to settle herself. "How do you think he's doing?"

I wished I had thought a moment before I blurted out, "Oh, great. He's taking it really well, I think."

They glanced at each other, troubled. It made me feel . . . not fake, exactly. Just aware of how much his cheery good mood bothered me, too. And how much I had tried to overlook it. He was still like that, yesterday. Except if anything came up about his eye he brushed it aside so nimbly I'd forget to get back to it. Here, watching his mother and father send worried looks to each other, I couldn't deny how creepy he had made me feel.

"Did he see any light today, when that doctor came in?" I asked. Mr. Bannister bit his lip and shook his head. The coffee cake sat before us, untouched. "When . . . when should he start seeing some light, there? How long does he have to wait?"

Mr. Bannister said, "They won't wait too much longer."

"Who, the doctors?" My voice trailed off. "They won't wait much longer for what?"

"If they don't get some vision in there soon," he said, "they'll . . . they'll . . ."

Mrs. Bannister helped him. "They'll have to take out the eye."

And now I understood why he'd been so edgy, so hyper. How else could he be, one step from that? "But he'll be blind, then, in that eye, won't he? He'll be blind."

Mrs. Bannister shielded her eyes with her hand. Her husband nodded. "They'll wait another five days or so, and then they have to take it out. It's all . . . it's ruptured, they said, right, honey?" Mrs. Bannister nodded. "The back of the eyeball is ruptured."

"Five days?" I saw Mrs. Bannister look up at me in surprise, and I felt myself shaking. "Why can't they wait? Maybe it'll just take some time. . . ."

"They don't have time." Mr. Bannister pulled a wrinkled slip of paper from his pocket. "He could develop . . ." He read from the paper, moving his lips, "Sympathetic . . ."

Mrs. Bannister leaned over his shoulder and finished for him. "Sympathetic opthalmia," she said.

Mr. Bannister shook his head and muttered, "I can never say that."

"It's something about antibodies." Mrs. Bannister looked to her husband for confirmation. "The bad eye forms antibodies . . . and they could harm . . . the good eye. . . ."

"The eyes work together," Mr. Bannister said, as if for a moment we were watching a science program on TV. "They're connected, and if one goes bad, the other follows suit." He slumped a little in his chair. "So they can't wait."

"Does Todd know that?" I asked hoarsely.

"As soon as he came to, and could understand, we told him."

"The doctors didn't say it was certain," Mrs. B. added. "They didn't want to take away any hope from the start. They said we'd have to wait and see."

The phone rang then, and rattled us all. Mrs. Bannister rose to answer it. Mr. Bannister and I glanced at each other, looked away, back again.

"Todd's a battler," I said to him. "He's tough as hell."

From the other room Mrs. Bannister's voice was cordial. "Yes, Mr. Gilbert, I remember you, from the Angels, of course . . . Yes, I know we had an appointment for Friday, but you see, Todd . . . Oh, you know. . . . Yes . . . No, of course not. Well, thank you. That's very kind of you. . . ."

I sat up straight and faced Mr. Bannister, and did my best to block out her words from the other room. "I'm not worried about Todd," I told him. "Not one bit."

Eleven days after the accident the doctors removed Todd's right eye. The Bannisters told me that night when I called. The only way to keep calm was to listen to every detail. That wasn't easy. Todd had to go under a full anesthetic. There were all these muscles the doctors had to take off the eyeball before they took it out, and then a plastic ball went in its place. They reattached the muscles to the ball, sewed the skin shut, and then put a piece of plastic, a prosthesis, over that to keep the shape of the eyelid. If all went well it would pass for a real eye in every way.

"Except, of course," Mr. Bannister added, as if reminding himself, "he won't see on that side."

It was another two days before he could take visitors. From the hospital corridor I looked into his open doorway. This time the lights were on, the blinds open. The shelf beneath the window was lined with flower arrangements and silvery Mylar balloons. Todd was lying still, as if asleep. A thick wad of bandages wrapped the right side of his head. The IV tube was still attached to his arm. I crept in, to check if he was awake, thinking I could always come back later. . . .

"I see you," he said. It made me jump, for he still hadn't moved, and it was as if his voice had come from somewhere else. "I see you. I'm not totally blind, you know."

Then he turned toward me. The bandages formed a little mound over the right eye, and looped his brow like a headband. A few tufts of hair sticking up over it made him look like a little kid with a cowlick. For a moment I was stuck there, unable to speak. But the bandages weren't what made my mouth go dry. It was the way he had said the word *blind.*

I gulped. "How are you feeling?"

"I feel like hell. All doped up." He made a motion to sit up, but seemed to quit halfway through. I thought back to the last time I had seen him, so fidgety and talkative. This was worse. His voice was sleepy, the words slurred. There was a chair on the other side, and I pulled it up to the bed. Too late I realized I was sitting on his right side, and he had to turn his whole head around to see me.

"They had me talk to a shrink," Todd snorted. "Before the operation." He imitated her voice. " 'How do you feel? Are you angry? Are you scared?'" Todd shook his head in contempt. "How do I *feel?* I'm losing my goddamn eye, how the hell does she *think* I'd feel?" He pushed himself up in the bed a little, and when he spoke again, his voice was faint. "It was such a waste of time they want me to see her again."

I had only talked to Todd just about every day for the last six years, but here, when I really needed to, my brain just sputtered. I asked if there were anything else the doctors had to do. I told him how many kids at school were going to come see him. He nodded. And then we sat for almost a minute, not saying anything. "So," Todd finally spoke. "Aren't you going to ask?"

"Ask?"

"Aren't you going to ask if I can still pitch?"

I drummed my fingertips along one thigh.

Todd waited. "How come you never asked?"

I squirmed in my chair. "I . . . uh . . ."

"You've been in to see me almost every day." He propped himself up higher. "How come you never—"

"I guess . . ." I would have said anything to stop this. "I guess I didn't think about it."

"You didn't *think* about it?"

I would have said anything, but what came out was the truth. I *hadn't* thought about it. Or, really, what I'd done was force it out of my mind, and that wasn't easy. Like over at his house, when Mrs. Bannister talked on the phone to that scout. Or at school, when people asked me, "How's Todd? Is he going to be all right?" What they were asking, I saw now, was *Will he still be able to pitch? Can he still make the big leagues?* No wonder I answered so quickly, "Sure, he'll be all right," and turned away.

We were all speaking in a kind of code that translated to *Don't ask and I won't have to tell you.*

And now Todd had abandoned the code.

"You're not the only one," Todd said. "It's like nobody wants to be the first to say it." I shifted under his gaze. "But I expected more from you, Paulie."

"I didn't think about it," I pleaded. "That other stuff, you know, pitching . . . that's way off. Everyone just wants you to get better."

"Get better," he droned.

"Sure. Hey, I was wondering, has Melissa been in—"

"Paulie, nobody's been here since they did the surgery except my mom and dad—and you. And how the hell did you get here so fast? What, were you waiting outside the operating room?"

"Melissa will be here," I said. "Probably this afternoon."

"Forget Melissa, okay, Paulie? Will you let it go with Melissa? Anyway, you think I'm looking forward to everybody coming in here and tiptoeing around the subject, pretending the whole idea of my never pitching again never even occurred to them?"

"I wasn't pretending—"

"I didn't say you, okay? I said everybody else—"

"Okay, okay. Maybe you can call down to the desk and say you're too tired for visitors."

"Yeah," he conceded, and slouched down in the bed. "You're right."

I looked at him lying there, his face drained, and I knew how much I'd rather have him yelling at me. "What the hell," I said. "Let's watch some TV."

"Nah. We don't have to. . . ."

"Come on. Let's rot our brains," I kidded. "Let's watch *Oprah*."

He gave in with a shrug, and turned to the table on his other side, where the remote lay next to the telephone. "I'll get it," I said, starting to rise, but he waved me away. And then, while I watched, his left hand reached out to the table as if the IV stand wasn't even there. His forearm hit the stand with a clang, knocking it to the table. The telephone rattled loose, the remote clattered to the floor, and the IV stand started to fall forward onto Todd.

I lunged across the bed to catch it. With one hand I cradled the plastic bag of fluid. "I'll call the nurse," I said.

"Paulie, relax." Todd helped me set the stand upright beside him. He glanced at his arm, and at the bag. "It's okay. I'm still plugged in."

"How do you know? Maybe you—"

"How do I know?" He gave a thin smile. "That's the second time today I've done that."

Part Two
THE HOT-STOVE LEAGUE

Chapter 7

No matter what Todd said, I wasn't bringing up baseball. Not after he told me how the letters and phone calls from the coaches and scouts dried up within three weeks. How the colleges that had sent him letters of intent, mini-contracts for scholarship athletes to sign, now sent carefully worded copouts that never once mentioned his eye.

Of course he never said not to talk about it, but what kind of friend couldn't see how much pain he was in every time he slammed down a letter—"Want a laugh? Read *this* one"—and turned away. I could see there was a difference between what he needed and what he thought he needed. And I wasn't about to sit there and watch him wince every time somebody mentioned baseball without thinking. So I let the World Series go by without ever once suggesting we watch an inning. And whenever he came back to school, I was ready to stand guard over every conversation that might harm him.

For a while I didn't have much of a chance at that. Todd stayed out of school a lot longer than he said he would. One day, then another, I waited for him at the corner where we always met to walk to school, but he didn't show. A couple of times I was even late to first period, but I wanted to be sure I didn't miss him. "Tomorrow, Paulie, tomorrow," he kept saying when I called him in the afternoon. After the fourth time my dad said I should probably stop asking.

He didn't come back till the end of October. I was out on the corner, about two seconds from giving up on him for the day and racing to class, when I saw him come shuffling up. "Here I am," he joked. "Just in time for Halloween."

I couldn't even force a laugh. I was too busy staring at those same dark glasses he had worn in the hospital, and I must have been obvious about it. "What's the matter?" he asked.

"Nothing, just—"

"What is it? The glasses? What's wrong with them?"

"Nothing's *wrong*. Just—I'm just surprised to see them. You weren't wearing them at home." I licked my lips. "I was wondering, how come—"

"How come I'm wearing them now?" He leaned in toward me, lifting the glasses and pulling down on his lower eyelid so I had a close-up of the dull gray ball where his right eye used to be. "Paulie, why do you think?"

Once we were at school, though, everybody flocked around Todd, happy just to see him. I knew that had to feel a lot better than the giant get-well card the senior class had sent him, or the phone calls, or even people stopping by his house. He must have been hugged three dozen times the first day alone, and Dr. Maethner, the principal, even welcomed him back on the morning announcements. The halls had always been Todd's personal kingdom, I realized; there had always been something special about the way the kids would just naturally step aside for him with a smile or a nod.

But the first day even I could see something was different. People would call, "Hi, Todd"—and he'd duck his head and flash an embarrassed grin. After lunch a couple of sophomore girls stopped to gush. Todd nearly always soaked that up, but not this time. He just smiled and kept going. And on Tuesday, just before ninth period, when we usually walked to our English classes together, he pulled up short just before the main hall and turned down the corridor toward the gym.

"Hey," I said. "Aren't you going to class?"

"Sure." He shrugged, fiddling with his glasses. "I just thought I might go this way. It's quiet."

"Quiet?" He had already started down the hall and I fell in step beside him. "Since when do you want *quiet.* . . ."

On Wednesday I knew the answer to that, when I saw him between second and third periods. At first it looked just like old times, a cluster of kids pressed against him at his locker. As I watched from the end of the hall, though, I could see something strange on his face. His head darted this way and that, he shuffled his feet uneasily while the kids jabbered, as if he were seeking a way to escape and there was someone blocking every path.

What I saw was panic. I heard it in his voice, too, for when he spotted me he called out my name as if he hadn't seen me in ten years and lurched toward me, eager to lose the crowd. I knew it couldn't have been easy, coming back. I should have just asked him if that was it—but I didn't. I didn't want to make him feel worse. He'd get used to it, I told myself. He just needed some time.

The next day, Thursday, he was out again.

He was back again on Friday, but the next week, when he wasn't back by Wednesday, I stopped over after school.

"It's those headaches," Mrs. Bannister whispered, leading me up the stairs to his room. "From all that reading."

"Oh, of course," I whispered, though how he was doing so much reading when he'd left his books in school since Friday I didn't ask. I cradled the load of texts I had grabbed from his locker before coming over.

Todd was leaning over his dresser, his face about two inches from the mirror.

"What's that?" He saw the pile of books in the reflection.

I dumped them on his bed. "Just some stuff I thought you'd need to—"

"Jeez, Paulie, you went into my *locker*? You're worse than my mother."

I ignored that. "You okay?"

He still hadn't turned my way. He was tinkering with something—at first, I thought, his glasses. But as I pulled the chair out from his desk, I spotted them: in the wastebasket, the lenses snapped apart, the temples twisted off.

"Paulie," he boomed the words out confidently. "It's time for a change." He turned to face me.

A large black patch covered his right eye.

I stared. I stared for too long. What was I supposed to say, *Nice patch?* Finally I motioned to the wastebasket and croaked, "What was wrong with the glasses?"

"Oh, nothing," he said. "I just got tired of people treating me like I'm blind." He turned back to the mirror. "Like I'm *totally* blind."

"Come on," I scolded him. "They do not."

"They *do.*" He raised his voice. "They hold doors open for me. And they let me go first, into rooms." Todd laughed sourly. "You know, people used to let me in the doorways first because I was the superstar pitcher. Now they let me in first because I'm a cripple."

"You're not a cripple."

"No," he said. "I'm worse. I'm dead now."

"Stop it."

"I was alive then. I'm dead now." He took two quick strides to his desk, opened a dictionary and withdrew a folded sheet of paper. "Listen to this. It's from Melissa."

"Melissa?" My voice brightened.

It took him a second or so to adjust the paper in front of him. " 'Dear Todd,' " he read aloud, " 'I want you to know how sorry I am that this had to happen to you. I'm not going to pretend that it's not going to be tough for you, but I want you to know that you'll always be one of my closest friends, one of the people I care most about, and I'm here for you when you need me.' "

Todd's voice was shaky on the last few lines. "That's . . . terrific," I said quietly.

"Uh-huh," he said, and glanced up. "Why a letter? Why didn't she just tell this to me?"

I shrugged. "I don't know."

"Because," he explained, "she didn't want to look me in the eye."

"Get out of here," I said. "She came to see you in the *hospital.*"

"I don't mean *that eye*," he snapped. "I mean my good eye. Haven't you noticed? She's just like all of them. When they get up close they never look me in the eye."

"Duh, Todd, it's because you've been wearing *sunglasses.*"

"I can see the wheels turning in their heads, 'He's blind now, he's blind,' they keep thinking, so they focus on my nose, or my hair—"

"You're just feeling sorry for yourself."

"They look anywhere, but not in my eye. It's like they're afraid what they'll *really* see inside me, so all they say is 'How are you, Todd?' "—he mimicked an airhead voice—" 'How's it going, Todd?'—"

"What are they *supposed* to say?"

"Or they don't say anything." He held up the note. "They send letters."

"You're wrong," I said.

"Am I?" I hated when he smirked like that.

"Well, you're wrong about Melissa."

He ignored that. "So, now I've got the patch." He folded the letter and replaced it in the dictionary. "I'll force them to look me in the eye."

"Listen," I said, "you've got to stop missing school. You've got to start concentrating on your classes."

"Oh, yeah?" He patted the patch back in place. "What are you, Mr. National Honor Society?" He glanced at the load I had thrown on his bed. "How come *you* don't bring home any books?"

"Don't worry about me," I said. "I'll get by."

"Well, I can get by, too." Suddenly his good eye glinted suspiciously. "Did Hedstrom tell you to say all this?"

"Hedstrom? Why would—"

"'Cause he wants me to take the SATs over." Todd crossed his arms and stared out the window. "You know, a month ago it was enough for any college in the country if I just wrote my goddamn *name* on the SATs."

Then he was back at his mirror, reaching for a red Cardinals cap from the edge of the dresser. It was one of the little "gifts" the scouts had sometimes left for him, even though, as an amateur, he wasn't supposed to take or sign anything. I remembered the way I just about drooled the first time he showed it to me—the deep red wool, the pure white letters, *StL*. A twenty-five dollar hat in the stores, and here somebody had just dropped it in his lap. He had a little trouble now slipping it on over the eye patch, but finally he faced me, the cap just so. "Hey," he said. "Can you see me on the Cardinals?"

Below the brim of the cap I saw the pale face with the black patch swooping across.

"I don't know," I said, and then some genius instinct in me tried to make a joke. "Maybe the Pirates."

But I'd gone too far, and I knew it instantly. "Is that supposed to be funny?" he snarled.

"Huh-uh," I said quickly. "I mean, I was just kidding. You asked me—"

"Never mind." He took one more look at the mirror, then pulled the cap off and threw it beside me on the bed. "You want it?"

"You're giving this to me?" I was almost afraid to pick it up. "Don't you want it?"

"For what?" he said sullenly.

"Come on," I cautioned him. "Don't start on—"

He ripped the patch off and turned on me. "But it's true, isn't it?" His face was livid, but for the lifeless right eye. "*Say it,*" he cried. "I used to be a big star—"

"Stop it," I yelled back, and then I said more. "Stop *hiding* in here."

He blinked, surprised, and the anger seemed to fade. "Hiding?"

"You ought to be in school, not moping around your room. The more you're around people—"

"Paulie—"

"—the less you'll be worried about what they *say,* or who holds a *door* open for you."

"You don't understand. . . ."

"You ought to go to a *party* or something."

"What are you *talking* about?" he yelped. "You hate parties."

"So who says I have to go? You go yourself. What, it'll kill you to have some fun?"

"I can't believe it." He half smiled. "Dr. Lockwood prescribing parties."

"Come on." I stood up. "Let's get out of here. Let's go somewhere." I should have suggested that long ago; why wouldn't he get depressed, holed up in that bedroom, surrounded by all those trophies and plaques?

"All right." He grabbed his jacket. "Hey, take the cap." He motioned to where it lay on the bed.

"Nah, that's okay."

"Take the cap."

I slipped it on—about half a size too big for me—and followed him down the stairs, feeling a little up for the first time in weeks. This is what he needs, I thought. Just to get out. At the busy corner near his house I paused for a gap in the traffic, then darted across the street—but Todd wasn't with me.

I looked back and saw him, still on the other side. He moved his head in a slow, deliberate motion, checking the cars in both directions with his good eye, the left eye. When there was finally a wide open space he trotted across and joined me. "I'm still a little nervous," he said sheepishly, "crossing streets."

Chapter 8

When I saw Melissa's car parked in front of the pharmacy, I took a deep breath, tried the handle—she never did lock it—and hopped in the passenger side. There I ducked low, pulling Todd's Cardinals cap over my brow, and propped my knee against the dashboard. I watched Melissa come out of the pharmacy, her face drawn, her hair tugged back with a scrunchie.

Two steps out the door she paused to light a cigarette.

"Paulie." She jumped in surprise when she saw me, then climbed behind the wheel. "I thought I was getting carjacked," she laughed.

"That's what you went in there for?" I said. She was still pretty, no matter how tired she looked. "For cigarettes?"

"Oh, give me a break, huh?"

"When did you start smoking again?"

She ignored that. "So how are you? You need a lift?"

"Me?" I made a big show of waving away the smoke. "I'm not going anywhere. Actually—I wanted to ask you about the SATs."

She made a face. "What about them?"

"Well—you did really great on them, right?"

She shrugged. "Fourteen hundred, around. Pretty good, I guess."

"*Pretty good?* That's like saying *Ted Williams* was pretty good."

Her face went blank. "Who's Ted Williams?"

I rolled my eyes. "Never mind. But since you did so well, you'd probably be able to help somebody who was—who was going to take them, right?"

She smiled curiously. "Are you asking me to help you with the SATs?"

"*No,*" I almost shouted, then added, quietly, "It's, uh, not for me."

"Who, then?" Suddenly she sat up and jabbed out the cigarette. "Paulie. Are you asking me to work with Todd?"

"Just for this one thing. . . ."

"Paulie . . ."

"Come on, Melissa, how hard would that be?"

"It *would* be hard. It'd be"—she shut her eyes—"awkward, that's what."

"So what? That's how I've felt my whole life." She tried to hold back a smile. "You know he needs better SATs to get in college."

"I know, I know."

"He had a hell of a bad break, Melissa."

"Of course he did. . . ."

" '*I'm here for you when you need me,*' " I said. "Remember that?"

Her eyes narrowed. "Where'd you get that from?" she demanded. "Did Todd show you my letter?"

"Huh-uh," I lied. "I just . . . saw it."

"Oh, so now you read other people's mail?"

"No. What do you think, I'm his mother? He had it lying right on his desk."

She turned away from me, her fingers drumming on the wheel. "Sorry. I can't do it."

I waited. And waited.

Finally she asked, "So how's he doing?"

"Todd?"

"Yes, Todd," she snapped. "Don't play dumb."

"He's . . ." All at once I felt exhausted, as if half of me had melted into her front seat. *How's he doing?* I didn't even know where to start. "He's all right."

"I heard he went to Lorrie Houston's party."

"Yeah." I tried to look positive. "He did."

"I heard he got drunk."

I shifted in the seat. "I heard that, too. . . ."

"Well what's he getting drunk for?" Her voice rose and she faced me. "That doesn't sound like Todd. How'd he start going to *parties?*"

"I guess . . . it was my idea. All I said was maybe he should get out once in a while. At least he's not just staying at home, moping around."

"Oh, sure, getting drunk is much better."

"I didn't say that."

"That's why you want me to help him with the SATs. You feel guilty."

"I do not." I thought of the stories that always circulated the week after a party. How so-and-so got nabbed by her parents crawling in a window at three A.M.; how four or five football players walked home from the last one with their shirts off, even though it was December. Todd never mentioned himself at any of them. He didn't have to. I could tell when I saw him the following Sunday, how hung over he was. I knew I wasn't responsible for his going to Lorrie Houston's and getting polluted, or going to Charlie Roach's the week before—I guess Melissa hadn't heard about *that*—but I did tell him to go out. I did mention parties.

And I did feel guilty. She was right.

I grabbed the armrest and the center console, hoisted myself up. "Melissa. We've got to help him through this."

She shook her head and looked away.

I kept on. "You know it's true. If you were still with Todd he wouldn't be getting drunk at parties."

"Stop." She leaned forward, resting her chin on the steering wheel.

"Melissa, all I'm saying is, for a while, couldn't you just . . . couldn't you . . ."

"Couldn't I be his girlfriend again?"

"*Yes.*"

She shook her head and lit another cigarette. "Paulie, that's not how it works."

"It could work. If you tried."

She took a deep drag. "No, Paulie. You can't live your life for another person."

"That's—" I reached for the door handle. "That's selfish."

"No, it's not. It's taking care of yourself. There's a difference."

I climbed out of the car, my muscles so knotted up I could hardly stand. "I just feel like, here when Todd needs our help, everybody's jumping ship."

"And you're the last man on deck."

"I guess I am."

"Paulie." She started the car. "Ships have lifeboats. There's a reason for that."

Every night Todd had to remove and clean the prosthesis that covered up where his eye had been. Usually he did that before bed, so I was surprised he was doing it now, at eight o'clock on a Saturday night. I sat across from him in his room and watched, though I tried not to look like I was staring. Todd didn't care. He'd been doing it for close to two months. He squirted a liquid on it, rinsed it off, held up his top lid and settled it in with the same nonchalance that my mother put in her contacts every morning. This was the third prosthesis, about an inch across; as the swelling of the muscles went down, the doctor replaced it with a larger size. When all the swelling was finally gone—the doctor said that would probably be around March—he would be fitted with the final prosthesis, and that one would be hand painted to match his left eye exactly.

Now he was almost done. He blinked gingerly, checked his eye in a small desk mirror, and then went off to the bathroom where the light was better.

He would only be gone a minute, so I lunged for the envelope that I had spotted when I first came in, the one from the New York Association for the Blind. I hunched over, slipped the letter out and unfolded it, my fingers trembling. Melissa was right, I thought. Now I *was* reading his mail.

Dear Mr. and Mrs. Bannister. I skimmed ahead, past the *Thank you for your interest* part, too jittery to read line by line. Instead, certain words jumped out at me. *Problems . . . understanding . . . adjustment.* I slowed down at *There are times when friends and family just may not be enough* and read that twice. In the next paragraph, *recommend . . . sliding fee scales . . . benefit plans . . . and two columns of doctors' names, addresses, phone numbers.*

But he's got a doctor, I thought. Then I heard Todd's steps in the hallway. I jammed the letter back in, laid the envelope on the exact spot where I'd found it, and leaned back in the chair, as if I hadn't so much as breathed since he'd left the room.

Friends and family just may not be enough.

That's when it came to me.

They were shrinks.

"So," Todd checked himself in the desk mirror and turned to me, "how do I look?"

Maybe I'd never get used to the plastic lens; it moved like his good eye, but not perfectly. There was the slightest drag, and I always noticed it. "You look . . . okay," I tried. "Fine."

"Don't worry," he said cynically, drawing the strap of the patch over his head. "I'm wearing this."

"What's that letter about?" I asked, nodding toward the desk. "That one from the New York Association for the Blind."

"What? That?" He hesitated. We looked at each other. I could feel my whole body inclining toward him to make it easier to say.

I wasn't ready for the ragged laugh. "Ah, that's nothing. Just a brochure on their new spring line of canes."

I waited for more, but there wasn't any. Todd leaned down to the desk mirror, adjusted the patch, patted down the edges, and stood up. "I guess it's time," he said.

What I should have said—*Don't joke about it. What's really in the envelope?*—I didn't. I settled for, "Why do you *go* to these things?"

"What do you mean," he pretended he didn't understand, "these *things?*"

"These parties," I said.

"Hey, Paulie," he bantered. "Excuse me. It's Saturday night. I'm an unattached eighteen-year-old high school male. What am I supposed to do?"

"You haven't gone to those kinds of parties since you were a sophomore."

"I know," he said. "I've got a lot of catching up to do."

"And you don't even *like* those people there, the real hard-core drinkers, with the kegs and that."

He grabbed his jacket. "They're okay. They're not so bad."

"See?" I jumped on it. "Not so bad? That's just it. You're better than those guys. You're special."

Todd grinned coldly. "Not anymore I'm not."

"*I don't get you,*" I said. "First you were missing school. And then when you did come you didn't want to see anybody. And now you're going to these stupid parties."

"You know why?" He stood at the door, his fist tight around his jacket. " 'Cause that didn't work, just going back to school. This works."

"Going out and getting drunk with guys like Tommy Ricco works?"

"Yeah. It helps me relax."

"Almost falling down the stairs at Charlie Roach's, that's *relaxing?*"

"How'd you know about that?"

"Not from you, that's for sure." I mumbled, "I overheard some guys at lunch."

"Well, see? It's something to talk about. I don't just have to stand around while people get all tongue-tied because they can't look me in the eye."

"Does getting drunk help them look?"

"No," his voice wavered. "It helps me not notice so much."

With that he hurried down the stairs. He called to his folks that he was leaving, and out in front of his house, where I would have turned to go home, we huddled for a moment against the cold. "All right." He tugged on his gloves. "I'll call you."

"What do you mean?" I said. "I'm coming, too."

"*You're* coming?" Todd looked pained. "You're coming to a party?"

"Hey," I mimicked him. "It's Saturday night."

Chapter 9

When we got to Danny Sheehan's house, everybody made a big fuss over Todd; I slipped in after him, unnoticed, and cringed. The air was smoky, the stereo was blasting, and certain bass notes plunged so low you could feel floorboards buzz in response. I followed Todd to the kitchen where he tapped himself a beer. Somebody tried to offer me one, and as I waved him away I lost sight of Todd for a second. Then I spotted him in the living room by the Sheehans' Christmas tree.

I didn't take more than two steps his way before Luther Henderson, the first baseman, had to alert everybody in the universe I was there with an exaggerated cry of surprise. *"Paulie Lockwood, damn.* What are you doing here? You getting wasted tonight?"

Only wasting my time, I thought, but I just nodded no.

"Hey, you like this music?" Luther grinned. "You gonna dance?"

Steve Bates came over, guzzling a beer. "Dance?" He leered into my face. "The only music Lockwood likes is 'Take Me Out to the Ball Game.'"

Everybody roared at that. Todd showed the thin line of a smile.

"I'm going to find something to eat," I called to him, and forced my way around a crowd of dancers. The only snacks were at a card table littered with some empty plastic bags, Doritos crumbs, and popcorn. But that was all right. It really wasn't food I was after anyway. It was Melissa.

I suppose I still hadn't given up on getting them together, no matter what she told me that day in her car. But after another circuit of the room I was certain there was no Melissa, and I picked my way back to Todd.

I found him in the kitchen, by the keg. He and Steve Bates and Tommy Ricco were playing buzz, and other kids were gathered around them, like spectators. Buzz was a drinking game, and though I had heard of it, I didn't really know the rules.

"Twenty-six," Todd counted, "twenty-seven." All at once the group cried, *"Buzzzz,"* with the mocking tone of *gotcha.* Todd slapped his hand against his forehead, grinned, and chugged down a plastic cup of beer.

"Twenty-eight, twenty-nine," Steve Bates took over, and instead of "thirty" he said "buzz," and instead of "thirty-three" he said "buzz" again. Gradually I began to understand the game. There were certain numbers you avoided saying, sevens and multiples of ten and double numbers like forty-four. You were supposed to say "buzz" instead. I watched in astonishment as Bates, who I always figured could hardly spell his name, reeled through the numbers with a satisfied grin. He blared with laughter when Todd or Tommy screwed up and had to drain a cup as "punishment."

"Hey," someone called. "Todd has to start over."

"Todd." I tried to motion to him, but he didn't notice.

"One, two, three . . . ," he began.

I rocked on my heels nervously. All around me kids were looking on, laughing.

". . . six, *buzz*," he emphasized, and the crowd cheered. "Eight, nine, *buzz*. . . ."

"Faster," Bates demanded.

He messed up on seventeen, though, forgetting to say buzz, and gulped down a cup. After Tommy and Bates went for a while it was Todd's turn again. This time he was worse. I could hear him slur the numbers more, and every time he didn't buzz and had to take a drink the kids hooted.

"*Todd*," I called louder, but there was too much noise for him to hear. People were packed in close. I turned away and someone took my spot immediately. It wasn't so much the game I couldn't stand—it was the crowd. Whenever Todd missed a buzz they cheered him. It was probably the first time they had ever seen him lose at anything.

I drifted to the living room, and found a spot on the edge of the sofa by the potted tree. Someone had put on the video of *How the Grinch Stole Christmas.* Everyone in the room was chattering and giggling. I heard "Remember this part?" and "I read this in *second* grade!" and "Check out that sleigh!"

I must have watched for ten minutes without paying any attention when suddenly I heard, "Derek Jeter."

The voice seemed muted and distant. Maybe the smell of all that beer was getting to me.

"Derek Jeter, 1996." There it was again.

I shook my head, the way you do when you feel a mosquito in your ear, and saw Chuckie Miles, smirking at me from across the room.

I said automatically, ".314, and ten homers."

"See?" Chuckie turned to the kid with red hair next to him. "Told you he'd know. Now pay up."

"Aw, double or nothing," the kid held out. He looked over. "Curt Schilling, 1995," he challenged me.

I sat up a little. "Seven and five, 3.57 ERA."

"Waah," Chuckie jeered. He turned back to me. "Randy Johnson, 1994."

I answered that one, too, of course. Maybe it was only because the Grinch video was over, but soon everyone in the living room was leaning toward me, even the girls, and firing the names of ballplayers. Chuckie stood up like an emcee. "He only knows the last seven years," he announced, but they were impressed anyway. "Mo Vaughn." "Mark Grace." I answered nonchalantly, and perked up my ears for the next one. It was the first time all evening that I felt a part of anything. "How do we know he's right?" someone asked, so Danny Sheehan went upstairs and fetched a shoe box full of his brother's baseball card collection. They yanked cards at random, and read the names. I rattled off the stats, and each time an exaggerated *"Woh"* burst from the kids.

And just as I was feeling really great, flinging back the numbers before they hardly got the name out, somebody called, "Will Clark." Then someone else said, "No, no, *Dick* Clark," and then the red-haired guy wheezed, "Clark *Kent,*" and then they all tried to outdo each other. "Elvis," said one. "Shaquille O'Neal," some smart guy contributed. "The Pope," yelled another. I could feel the smile faltering on my face as some wandered off, and a few started searching for another video, and in no time I was there where I had started, on the edge of the sofa, alone again.

I got up to find Todd and get out of there. He was still in the kitchen with Bates and Tommy Ricco and a couple other seniors on the team. They were through playing buzz, but I only had to hear a few words from Todd to know how drunk he was. Perspiration beaded his forehead. His cheeks were bright red, and he was breathing through his mouth.

"Maybe you've had enough," I said.

He looked surprised to see me. "Where the hell you been?"

"Probably hitting on the women," Bates snorted. "Right, Lockwood?"

I should have just ignored them and tried to maneuver Todd out the door. "Ah, some people were trying to stump me on statistics," I said. "They were—"

"*That's* what you oughta do," Todd blurted suddenly. "You oughta be a . . . a statissss . . . a stati*stician.*" The reek of his breath could have knocked me over.

I took his arm. "Right," I said, "me with my C minus in math," and nudged him in the direction of the back door.

"What *are* you going to do?" he asked, as serious as you could be, that drunk.

"What do you mean?" I grumbled. Over my shoulder, Bates refilled Todd's cup with some beer from his own.

"If you're not going to be a statistician. What are you going to do?"

"What are *you* going to do?" I shot back. I shouldn't have, I know. I didn't even have the excuse of being drunk. You could almost hear the word I left off—What are you going to do *now*? It was the closest I'd come to mentioning pitching in more than a month.

Tommy Ricco and Bates went silent. I waited while Todd formed his lips around the words.

"I'm gonna . . . ," he began, then shook his head and blinked.

I waited. Todd began to sway, but his good eye never left my face. He swallowed with difficulty. "I'm gonna . . ."

Then Tommy grabbed Todd's arm and held it aloft. "He's gonna get *loaded*," he brayed, the beer sloshing from their cups. "He's gonna get bombed, right?"

"That's right." Todd laughed, and when he and Bates and Tommy went to clink their plastic cups together like the Three Musketeers, the cups caved in. I scooted aside as the beer gushed down around us. They cackled, cheered, and raised their cups again, and in all that time Todd never looked at me.

"Jesus, what a mess," Tommy said, looking down at the puddle at his feet. "Bates, you better clean this up."

"Yeah, right." He pointed to me. "What about Lockwood? He's the closest thing we got to a water boy."

I said, "Do it yourself," and kept my eyes on Todd.

"Wohhh," Bates pretended to cringe. Then he turned back to Tommy Ricco. "Hey, why don't you do it?" The two of them swore at each other for a while before they staggered off together to tell Danny Sheehan the kitchen floor looked like a lake.

Todd sipped down what was left in his cup, crumpled it and glowered at me. "Happy you came?"

"Let's go," I said. "You don't need any more." I picked up our coats from the chair in the corner and motioned him toward the back porch. We could slip out that way, and avoid the hurrahs of his fan club out front. But Todd had planted his feet and I couldn't budge him.

"Come on," I insisted. "You'd better get home." For a second I thought I had pried him loose, but he only shrugged me off.

"Watch it," he growled, as if I were some stranger who had bumped against him in a crowd.

I shook my head. "You're a jerk," I grunted, and this time locked hands on both his shoulders to wrench him from his spot. I didn't get far.

"Leave me the hell *alone*," he muttered. He drew up his hands and drilled me in the chest with a solid shove that sent me into the counter.

I lunged to shove him back, but he was quicker; he shot the heel of one palm against my chin. Shuffling for balance, I toppled backward into the puddle of beer, and then my feet slid out from under me. My head crashed into the cabinet beneath the sink. When I reached down to brace myself, I was already soaked.

I clutched the side of the sink and hauled myself up, cursing him out. But he wasn't listening. His face was yellowish white. He had one hand on the table and the other on the top of the keg, and it didn't look as if either were going to prop him up for long.

"So stay," I said. "The hell with you." But as I stepped around him to get my jacket I saw him push off and shamble toward the porch, bent over like a hunchback. There was a kind of desperate slow motion to it, as if he were plowing through a tub of gelatin. He banged a shoulder into the molding beside the door, fell back, and stumbled through.

"Hey," I called. "You all right . . . ?"

Out on the porch Todd crouched forward on his hands and knees, getting sick all over himself.

"Oh, jeez," I said. I threw aside my coat and took one uncertain step toward him.

When he heaved again, the odor wafted in my face. I winced and held back, as he rolled over on his side. I saw the vomit on his shirt, in his hair, along the eye patch and the side of his face. He laid his head down in it, breathing slowly.

Let him be, I told myself. This is what he deserves. And a part of me wanted to get down to his level and sneer, *Are you happy now?*

I watched him struggle to his feet only to pitch forward and throw up again. And this time, when he stopped, I picked my way past him, to the porch door.

My mistake was looking back. Todd fumbled around, first making it to one knee, then the other. A hand groped for support, and he managed to rise erect for a moment before he crumpled to his knees.

Halfway down the back steps, I lingered. And for an instant it wasn't Todd I was watching; it was me. At the school carnival, long ago, in my water-logged clown suit. In that same curled up shape, all dizzy and confused, reaching for something to cling to, and stay afloat.

Then Todd's firm grip on my arms, yanking me from the water tank.

Now, on the Sheehans' back porch, he was having trouble even rising to his knees, and I knew I wasn't mad at him anymore. I wasn't mad at the kids, either, Tommy Ricco or Bates, the ones who got him so drunk. They didn't mean any harm. If I left, one of them would probably find him, and clean him up, and help him home.

But I couldn't be sure.

"All I know is," I said, returning to the porch, "it's a goddamn good thing you came and pulled me out of that tank."

Todd croaked. "Wha . . ."

I hunted through some cupboards, grabbed a pack of paper napkins and did my best to wash his face and wipe the vomit out of his hair. It took a while to get him standing. He teetered before me, but I grabbed his forearms firmly and kept talking to him. Once I thought he was strong enough to walk, but as I slipped his coat on and turned him toward the door he collapsed against me. I stood him up and tried all over again. I hefted one of his arms over my shoulder and together we staggered to the back stairs. Each step was a labor, but I didn't care. If I had to help him home from a hundred parties, I'd do it, until he got through this. I'd hover in the background and watch over Todd as if I were his own private guardian angel. And if he woke up in the morning with his head buzzing but no memory of how far he'd fallen, well, I guess I'd be doing my job.

Chapter 10

Todd went to a few more parties after the one at Danny Shee-han's, but they couldn't have been much fun. Not with me there, watching whether he drank. Easing in when someone offered him a ride home so I could smell the driver's breath and see if it was safe. I was ruining the parties for Todd, and I was glad. At any moment I expected him to tell me to go to hell and leave him alone, but he didn't. And soon enough, when he was staying home on Friday and Saturday nights, as if he never really wanted to go to those things in the first place, I did my best to be there with him.

He stopped wearing the eye patch, too. I didn't ask him about it, the first time I saw him at school that way. I told my-self, What's the big deal?

What was tough was watching other kids react to it. You could see when somebody got close how his glance would get stuck on Todd's fake eye. He might try not to stare, he'd look away, but then get self-conscious of *not* looking, so he'd try to face him again, and all that time uneasiness would flicker across his face. Todd just had to notice. I sure did.

It didn't take me long to realize that although he wasn't

missing school anymore, he wasn't really at school either. He still kept taking those long routes to get to class, like past the gym or through the basement hall where the boiler room was. At lunch, he was never in the cafeteria, where it seemed he used to *own* a table. Sometimes I'd find him in the back corner of the library; sometimes he'd be hunched over a stack of college catalogs in the guidance office waiting room.

I wanted to yell at him then, *Where the hell have you been?* But I held back. I held back, I knew, in a lot of ways. For Christmas I almost always gave him a book or a video about baseball. This Christmas I got him a sweater. A nice sweater, sure, but all I thought when he held it up and said how much he liked it was that both of us knew this Christmas was different. There were times I wondered if I wasn't just like the other kids, afraid to mention his eye, afraid to even talk at all. I'd get angry then, scold myself, as if it were up to me to lead him in the right direction.

Except I didn't know what the right direction was.

So I'd take a seat right by him in the guidance office, say, "What's up, how you doing?" and pretend not to notice he wasn't really concentrating on those college catalogs he was leafing through. He was piling up a stack of them, as if, when they were high enough, he could scrunch down and hide so even I couldn't find him.

I stood in the software shop at the mall and stared at the displays. *Windows. Macintosh. CD-ROM.* I had a headache from the moment I stepped in. The tinny sounds of racing cars, laser blasters, dribbled basketballs, thuds and oofs and shrieks from all the computer screens drilled through my skull. Maybe those news reports were right, video games did cause aggressive behavior. Five minutes in the store and I was ready to kill.

When I heard the voice at my elbow, "What are *you* doing here?" I spun defensively. There stood Melissa in sweats and a leather bomber jacket, her hair bunched up in back.

"Oh no." I frowned. "Not you, too."

"What?"

I couldn't get over how good she could look without even trying, so I gestured to the shelves with contempt. "You, Melissa. In one of these stores."

She laughed. "Paulie, I've never known anyone so spooked by computers as you."

"Yeah, well, I've got to return something I got Tyler for Christmas. Then I'm getting right out."

"Christmas was three weeks ago," she teased. "You really rushed right over."

I looked at the box in my hand, *Myrtrano the Mind Invader.* "I don't know, I got him the wrong kind. Tyler's computer uses a different window, or something."

"Paulie," Melissa said. "How much do you know about computers?"

I waved her off. "I know plenty."

She looked at the box in my hand and led me over to another shelf. "Here." She took a new *Myrtrano* down and gave it to me. "He needs this Windows version."

"Thanks," I said. "God, I hate these places. I—"

"How's Todd?" she asked.

"Todd's great," I said quickly, and nodded. "He's doing fine."

If only she had just smiled and said, That's good. Then I could have exchanged the game and got out of there. But she was still watching me.

"You know," I gave in a little, "I mean, he's okay."

"He's lost a lot of weight, hasn't he?"

"I don't know. I guess. . . ."

"He hasn't just lost weight, he's *gaunt*, and when I see him in the hall—"

"Well, maybe," I snapped, "if everybody wouldn't *look* at him so much . . ."

"When I see him he's always ducking down, trying to avoid me—trying to avoid anybody—"

"Melissa," I said, louder than I meant to be, "why don't you just lay *off*, okay?"

"Paulie. How is he really?"

I sighed, and remembered from biology how a Gila monster, once he chomped into your leg, never let go, even after you cut off its head. There was a little Gila monster in Melissa for sure. "He's . . ." I tried to glance away, but felt her pulling back my gaze. "Melissa," I said. "I'm screwing up."

"Screwing up? What do you mean?"

"Because he's not going out and getting drunk, okay? And he's not missing school. And I'm doing everything I should be doing, and . . . and it's still not the same. He's not the same Todd."

"Paulie." She laid a hand on my arm. "How could he be?"

"I know," I said, feeling as if I were going to cry, right there, the worst place in the world for it, a computer store. I sniffed hard. "I'm his friend, goddamn it."

"Of course you are. Todd knows that—"

"But what kind of friend am I? I should be helping him through all this. But he's lost, Melissa. He doesn't know what to do."

Her lips pursed, but she didn't speak.

"You've got to help me," I said. She started shaking her head. "You've got to. I mean, you're his girlfriend, and—"

But at *girlfriend* her eyes raged. She turned and stomped off. I almost chased her out of the store, both boxes of *Myrtrano* under my arm. "Melissa, wait," I called, and leaped to the counter. It took the clerk about eight years to make the exchange, but when I rushed outside Melissa was still there—her arms folded tightly, purposely not looking my way—but still there. Well, that's something, I thought.

"Okay," I puffed, hurrying up to her. "I'm sorry, I—"

"I'm going to repeat this," Melissa said, "until you get it straight. I'm not his girlfriend."

"All right. But I need you to help."

She measured out each word suspiciously. "Help you how?"

We were at the center of the mall now. Some workmen up on ladders were taking down the Christmas decorations, tossing six-foot candy canes and tin soldiers into big cardboard boxes below.

"I guess . . . I don't know how," I said.

I felt her studying my face. "Paulie, it's only been three months. You have to give him some time."

Ahead of us the big glass elevator descended from the upper level.

"His life is different," she went on. "If I was going to be some superstar, and I'd been in all those magazines, and I was going to make millions of dollars, and then it was over, like that, and I had to get used to not being able to see on my right side—I'm not so sure I'd even be *back* at school by now."

There was a mob by the elevator, parents with little kids crashing their strollers into each other. "Forget this," she said, and we headed for the stairs. When she asked if I needed a ride home, I grunted yes.

"Look, I don't want to get involved, okay?" She shivered, one big frustrated twitch. "My life is really a mess right now. The newspaper's driving me crazy."

"I know," I said. "That last issue really stunk."

"Thanks. Thanks a lot."

"*Marching Band to Get New Uniforms,*" I kidded her. "God, who cares? You should have more sports."

"I'd love more sports. I'd love more sports*writers.* Do you know who I had to assign the last basketball game to? Donna Polara."

"The one who writes that *fashion* column?"

Melissa nodded painfully. "Wait till you see her article on the game," she groaned. " 'The Panthers definitely looked sharp in their stylishly trim jerseys of periwinkle and gold—' "

"Periwinkle?" I started gagging right outside Radio Shack. "They're grayish blue, not *periwinkle*. Jeez, Melissa, you've got to get somebody else."

"Oh, sure." She yanked back on her ponytail. "It's that easy, right? Just go out and—hey." I looked over to find her staring at me. "What about you, Paulie?"

"Me?"

"Why not? You know more about sports than *anybody*."

"Me. Sure. I can hardly write my name."

"All right." She looked at her watch. "Forget it. Dumb idea. Just don't criticize, okay?"

"Okay," I agreed. But suddenly I wasn't listening. Somewhere up the stairs the idea had hit me, and as it ricocheted through my brain I struggled to grab hold and get a clear look. It wasn't enough to keep Todd from the parties, or holing up in odd corners of the school like some recluse. It wasn't enough not to let anything *bad* happen to him—he needed something good.

I peeked at Melissa's profile, and turned away again.

Sure, she had told me loud and clear, no more *girlfriend* talk. I wouldn't dare bring it up, but it was obvious she noticed him, she looked at him, she cared—*he's gaunt, Paulie. He's avoiding me.* If I could only work something out, really *do* something . . . and they got back together—even for a while. . . .

But I had to do something quick. Once she gave me that ride home, when was the next time I'd even be *around* Melissa to make anything happen?

"What I know," I said, when we were almost at her car, "is *baseball*. I know a lot about baseball. Not other sports."

"So just write about baseball. Aren't they building a new practice field out behind the school? Write about that, okay?"

"You're crazy," I scoffed, but I didn't say no.

"Just baseball," she assured me, and smiled slyly. "After all, I've got Donna Polara for the rest."

Chapter 11

Melissa must have heard me swearing at the computer. Just about everybody in the library had. But she played innocent and only asked, "How's it going?"

"It's going great," I muttered. "I still wish you had let me write this with a pencil."

"I told you, this way I can edit it and put it right into the layout. So what do you think? You like using the computer?"

"Oh yeah. I like it a lot."

Why don't you tell her the truth, Paulie, that you could hardly walk into the school computer room without gagging. That you ducked in and out three times, lingering by the door like Steve Bates outside a liquor store, working up the nerve to pass himself off as twenty-one.

She leaned over to glance at the screen. "Can I see?"

"*No.*" I threw my hands up to cover it.

"Paulie." She pulled back. "What's wrong with you?"

Only a couple of other kids turned at my outburst. The rest tapped away at their keyboards, glassy-eyed.

"Nothing." My hands slipped from the monitor, and I could feel her reading the text.

"Uh, Paulie," Melissa said gently. "Can I make a suggestion?"

I looked at the screen:

This spring thAT OLDFIELD BEHIND
the school they never
used for anything except in the spr
ingthe art classes would go out there AND SKETCH
TREE STUMPS
and stuff is going
to be a practice field for the baseball te
am the games will still be at Portage Park but

"This isn't"—she bit back a smile—"supposed to be a poem, is it?"

"Ha ha. I'm screaming with laughter."

"Sorry," she said. "Look, do this." She reached across me and pressed a few keys. The words rearranged themselves as I watched. "There. That looks better, doesn't it?"

"Yeah," I grumbled. "Now it just stinks."

"Don't be like that. Just work on it."

I shrugged and rolled my chair closer.

She sat down beside me. "You're doing those interviews I told you to, right?"

I sighed for effect. "I'm talking to everybody I can," I said, and that was almost the truth. Mostly what I did was go out after school when nobody was around and walk all over the site of the new field, over the half-frozen clods and the big mounds of fill, trying to figure where second base would be.

"Just do a good job, then," Melissa said. "You know, we ought to think of a name for your column."

"My *column?*" I turned so quickly I must have leaned on the *page down* key. By the time I noticed, the screen was roaring ahead like a runaway truck.

Melissa fixed it. "That's what you're writing, a column. You need a name for it. *Baseball Report,* or something catchy, like, *Lockwood's Lockup.*"

"Yuck," I shivered. "Hey, I know. It's winter, right? So how about we call it *The Hot-Stove League?*"

"The Hot-Stove League. What's that?"

I stretched back on the chair. "That's what they called it, in the old days, in the winter, in these little hick towns. The old guys would chew tobacco around a potbellied stove and talk about who was going to be better next season, the Yankees or the Red Sox, and ..."

I glanced up to find Melissa staring at me.

"Why," she asked, puzzled, "would anybody do something like that?"

I shook my head. "Excuse me," I said. "I've got an article to write."

There are many good advantages, I typed, *to the new practice field. ...*

It seemed like the first time Todd had laughed in months.

" '*Good advantages,*' " he cackled, the school paper in his hand. " '*Many good advantages.*' "

Too bad it was my article he was laughing at.

"That's great, Paulie. Hey, why didn't you say, 'many *excellent* good advantages'?"

"All right, all right. . . ."

"Or better yet, 'many *super* excellent good advantages. . . .' "

"Hey, look," I tried to yank the paper from him, "just don't read it if it's so bad, okay?"

"And this part." He turned sideways so I couldn't reach and ran his finger down the page. " *'It looks like the infield will be filled in with some yellow loose crumbly stuff. . . .'* "

He turned back to me. " *'Loose crumbly stuff.'* I love it. It's so *technical.*"

"Thanks," I said. I crossed my arms and put my feet up on his desk. "It's awful, is that it?"

He wriggled. "No, it's just . . ."

Of course it was awful. I knew that. When I first saw the newspaper in homeroom and hurriedly turned to my column, even I could tell how bad it was. There was hardly a class all day where somebody didn't quote a line in jest.

By the time I found Melissa I was livid. "How could you let that be printed?" I yelled at her. "What kind of editor *are* you?"

"Paulie," she said, "I can add a comma here or there, or cut a paragraph—"

"You should have cut the whole damn thing," I sputtered.

"Are you mad I used it just like that?"

"Of course I am."

"Good. Maybe next time—"

"Next time?" I snorted. "Ha. That's it. I quit."

But I couldn't, of course. Not yet.

Now Todd was reading my article again, trying—not that hard, I thought—to hold back a grin. "You're going to write another one?" he asked.

"Ehh," I muttered. "Melissa said I—"

"You know, Paulie," Todd interrupted, "maybe *you* ought to go out with Melissa. You spend enough time with her."

"What are you talking about?" I stood up and took a step toward him. "I ought to deck you for saying that."

"It's true. It's so obvious you're in love with her."

"Just shut the hell up."

I glanced down to see my hands, already knotted into fists. Todd was half a head taller than I, and probably could have tossed me through the window if he wanted to. He didn't even look upset. I let my fists fall to my side, a little ashamed. "What I am," I said, "is *loyal.*"

Todd scratched his head. "What are you loyal about? It's over with Melissa and me. Forget about it."

"I'm just watching over her, okay?" I turned away from him, and mumbled, "In case you two get back together."

"You're watching over Melissa. You're watching over me." I saw a reflection of his face in the glass of a framed article on the wall. "Who the hell's watching over Paulie?"

One of the math teachers had had the bright idea of starting a Hackers Club in the computer room at lunch. All that meant to me was it guaranteed I could find Tyler there at least once a day. Sure enough, he was in the corner, using a mouse to doodle rainbow lines all over the screen.

110

"Listen." I sat down next to him. "I need you to do me a favor."

He nudged his glasses back up on his nose and stared at me. "Why should I?"

"Why? Because—" I wanted to shout *I'm your older brother, that's why,* but I knew that wouldn't work. "Tyler, remember when you were telling me," I lowered my voice, "that you could send messages on the computers. . . ."

He sat up in the chair, intrigued. "Sure. That's e-mail. Where do you want to send it? Tokyo? California?"

"How about across the room?"

"Across *this* room?"

I nodded. He half laughed, as if I'd insulted him, swiveled around on his chair, and surveyed the other kids. "Watch this." He turned back to the keyboard and tapped furiously. His screen blipped to black and then red. He looked like a guy in one of those old werewolf movies, caught out in the full moon. His tongue dangled and his eyes gleamed. "All I've got to do is get into SYSOP."

"SYSOP?"

"I told you, remember? How I changed that teacher's password? And then I—"

"Oh yeah," I surrendered. "I remember."

"Okay." He whispered out of the side of his mouth. "See that kid over there?"

A gangly kid twitched and shifted in his seat, dodging laser blasts from the computer.

"Yeah. So?"

"Keep watching—and let me know if any teacher comes in

here." Then he hit a flurry of keys, and suddenly the kid sat upright and peered in at the screen. In a second he turned around, scanning the room until he saw Tyler.

"Real funny, Lockwood," he said, and flashed him the finger.

Tyler was hysterical beside me. "Look." He elbowed me and pointed to his monitor. "Look what I wrote."

Kevin is a boner brain.

I sighed and rested my forehead in my hand.

"What's the matter?" Tyler asked.

"Sometimes," I said, "I forget you're a freshman."

"Is that what you want me to do?"

"That's the idea. Can you show me how?"

"Wait a minute." Tyler stared at me. "You want to do this *yourself?*"

"How long will it take me to learn?" I asked.

"You, Paulie?" Tyler pretended to calculate. "About ten years. Why don't you just give me the message?"

So much for keeping Tyler out of this. What I wanted, I told him quietly, was for Melissa to get a message on her computer—a message from Todd.

"I thought they broke up," he said.

"They didn't really *break up*," I hissed.

"And how come Todd isn't asking me? How come he doesn't just send roses?"

"You'll understand it when you get older." Could he send the message third period, I asked, when she was always in here working on the newspaper? And could he—

"Third period is *perfect*," he bellowed. I could barely keep from gagging him. "I can get here from study hall. Now—what do you want it to say?"

That stalled me. "Uh . . . how about . . ." I tore some paper from a printer and scribbled something, crossed it out, tried two more times before I handed it over.

" 'Melissa,' " Tyler read aloud, " 'I still love you, Todd.' "

"*Shhh,*" I said through gritted teeth.

"Isn't that," he wondered, "kind of . . . *schmaltzy?*"

"It's love, all right? You can get away with being schmaltzy."

Tyler folded the paper, tucked it into a notebook, and peered at me. "Todd doesn't know anything about this, does he?"

"He . . . knows enough. Look, can't you just send it?"

"I can send it. I just don't get why he needs you to straighten out his love life."

"He doesn't *need* me—"

"Then why?"

I think it was the edge of a grin that got me, Tyler sitting there as if we were bickering over some chore at home. But instead of yelling at him, I felt the air wheeze out between my teeth.

"Because," I said softly, "the poor guy's got nothing."

I'd only said what had been buzzing around my head for months, like some fly that singles you out and won't give up no matter how much you bat it away.

The poor guy's got nothing.

It wasn't easy saying it. Especially not with Tyler there, just enough of a witness to make me feel like some kind of traitor to Todd for even thinking that. Still, I wanted to go through with it. Tyler and I made our plans for third period the following Friday. I knew Melissa would be editing some articles, and from the other side of the room I could angle my chair to watch her while Tyler sent the message. I'd memorize every shiver, maybe even spot some tears. Give her a few days to go to Todd on her own, and when he'd mention it to me, I'd fill him in on the rest: how she looked, how obvious it was she cared, how they never should have been apart.

On Friday she was there, right on time. I waved to her from across the room. "Now let's wait a little," I whispered to Tyler. "Give her a chance to get settled."

I noticed the footsteps first, the way scouts in old cowboy movies put their ears to the ground and heard the sound of buffalo hooves. And it was like that, a stampede, when two dozen freshmen thundered through the doorway. Some raced for the best computers, others looked for friends to sit beside. Mrs. York, the earth science teacher, followed them in. Usually when a teacher brought a class to the computer center you were supposed to leave unless there were some leftover seats. She took less than a second to glance at Melissa, Tyler, and me, smirked, and then ignored us. That was all I could remember from her class, that smirk; it was always on her face, as if the whole point of her going to college and becoming a teacher was so she could correct you on *stalactite* and *stalagmite.*

"Did you know there would be a class in here?" Tyler asked me.

"This is even better," I said. "With this crowd Melissa won't know I'm watching."

I made him wait a few more minutes. Mrs. York was trying to get the kids excited about continental drift. "Okay." I poked Tyler. "Do it."

He lunged for the keyboard; it clicked beside me like chattering teeth. I squinted across the room at Melissa.

"Okay," he muttered to himself. "SYSOP . . . highlight work station . . . Hey." He turned to me. "You want it to beep?"

"What?"

"To get her attention. You want it to beep?"

"Sure. Make it beep. Just hurry up."

He went back to the keyboard, happy. "Enter message. . . ." I heard the keys sound out each letter. He leaned back, glanced at me, dusted off his hands, said, "Done," and pressed one final key.

There were close to thirty computers there, and all of them beeped at once. I took a glimpse at mine, instinctively, and then a longer look.

The screen had gone black. At the bottom I read: *Melissa, I still love you. Todd.*

"Hey, dummy," I jabbed Tyler. "You sent it to the wrong computer. You sent it to mine."

Then the whole earth science class cheered, and just as quickly went silent. I looked around the room and saw all the screens, black as mine, with the same strip of white lettering at the bottom. Mrs. York, sighing noisily, leaned over shoulders, tapped at keys. From around the room there were growing murmurs.

"Uh," Tyler said, typing furiously, "something's, uh, wrong here. . . ."

Melissa, still as a sculpture, stared at her screen.

115

I heard a giggle, but only one. Mostly just the *s-s-s* of hurried whispers. Twenty-four freshmen heads peeked around until they spied Melissa.

"It's on *everybody's* screen," I hissed at him. "Can't you fix it?"

"Well," he stammered, "I can, uh, I might be able to. . . ."

Mrs. York marched around the room. "Who's playing games? Who's the funny one?"

Melissa kneaded her fingers uneasily. She only looked up once, and when she did she caught two or three kids watching her. Suddenly she pushed back her chair, grabbed her book bag, and stormed out.

"I'm sure," Tyler whispered, "I can fix this. . . ."

"Never mind," I droned. Now the kids were starting to chatter, but I could hardly hear them—in my ears there was a roaring, like a hurricane on the way.

"Todd's going to kill you," Tyler said.

"*You* sent the message. *You* screwed it up."

Tyler bit his lip and shook his head. "He's going to kill you."

Chapter 12

I wished he *would* have killed me. But it was worse than that.

He didn't care.

"Paulie, why don't you stop worrying?" That was all he said. When I tried again, babbling all sorts of apologies, he still shrugged it off. "Don't do me any favors," he joked. *Joked.*

Still I kept on, *"I'm sorry, I'm sorry,"* and blaming as much on Tyler as I could, and this time he made it into something out of Aesop's *Fables.* "See what happens when you don't mind your own business?"

"I know," I said. "But . . . aren't you even mad?"

He didn't answer that. He just said, "How'd Melissa take it?"

I had to stop and sift through what happened. At first all I could think of was how she had ambushed me at my locker later that day, her eyes wild. She said a lot of nasty things, but the nastiest came when she calmed down. "You're really not being his friend, you know."

No way was I telling Todd that, so I tried to laugh it off. "Aw, Melissa's too smart for her own good," I said. "Half the things she called me I had to look up in the dictionary."

Todd chuckled softly.

"Oh, and she, uh, made me promise I'd write another, um, article . . . for the newspaper."

"Oh no." Todd cringed in mock horror. "*Son* of Hot-Stove League."

"Shut up."

"Look," Todd said. "For the last time. Let Melissa lead her own life, okay?"

"Okay, okay." Then I had a flash of all the kids in the whole school thinking they knew everything about Todd and Melissa, and snickering at how my trick had backfired. I grabbed his sleeve and pulled him to a stop. "But don't you want to, I don't know, even yell at me?"

His face was serene. "Would that make you feel better?"

"I guess not." But didn't he understand? How I felt wasn't the point.

A couple of evenings later I went over to see him. "What's up?" I hollered, as I saw him come down his front steps. He jumped at the sound of my voice.

"Jeez, take it easy," I kidded him. "What'd you think, you were getting mugged?" He managed something that wasn't quite a smile. "So where're you going?" I asked.

He glanced down at the ground, then up at me, then off. "Uh," he thought for a second, "the library."

"What is it, research paper?" He nodded quickly. "What the hell," I said. "I'll go with you."

Todd squinted for a second, the way you look when you're

trying to remember if you've left a faucet on in the house. "Okay," he said. "Yeah, I don't care."

"Hey," I teased, "don't knock yourself out thanking me." But this was a good sign, I told myself. At least he was getting out.

"Hey, where's your stuff?" I asked. "Your books, and—"

"Paulie, it's a library. They've got the books." But before I could say, Well, what about paper and pens and those index cards the teachers rave on about, he said, "I don't see you with any books."

"Don't worry about me," I answered.

"You can afford to just hang out at the library for a night without doing any homework?"

"I'm not hanging out," I said. "I'm waiting for you."

Todd looked concerned. "You ought to go home, get some books. I'll still be there."

"Nah." I twitched uncomfortably. "Besides, I didn't bring anything home from school."

"See?" he almost shouted. "Paulie, you're going to screw up all your classes."

"So what." I laughed it off. "How could anybody tell?"

Of course, I had a research paper, too, a week overdue at that, and I hadn't even picked a topic. So when we got to the library I left Todd at the newspaper microfilm desk and trudged down to my favorite section, 796.57, the only part of the Dewey Decimal System I knew by heart—the baseball books. I pulled down a title or two and pretended to search for something to write about, but my mind wasn't on it. Soon I stopped kidding myself. I was there, as I was everywhere, to keep an eye on Todd. I slouched on a stool at the foot of the shelves, and through a gap in the books I could see him, threading a spool of microfilm at the viewing machine.

And then I thought how there was something I couldn't protect him from, no matter how vigilant I was.

Usually by now, the middle of February, I was calling Todd up on the first halfway sunny day, trying to convince him to toss the ball around. *Practice'll be starting soon,* I'd say. This year was different. This year I never wanted the winter to end.

A book slid from my hand and thudded on the floor. I must have dozed off for a second. I whispered a sheepish curse, just grateful nobody had seen me. And then I sensed something different—the silence. There was no sound from the spinning microfilm. I shoved aside a couple of books to see. Todd was still at the viewing machine, frozen in front of the oversize monitor. He stared at something on the screen, his head arched forward. I squinted; his face seemed waxy and way too still.

He was so stuck on whatever was up there he didn't even hear me approach.

From over his shoulder I saw a grainy photo of a ballplayer, a kid in his late teens with a deep stare, as if he'd never trusted cameras.

"What's this?" I said.

Todd turned slowly, his face numb. He motioned to the article next to the photo. "Check it out."

My eyes left him, hesitantly, and I read the headline: *Prominent High School Pitcher Takes Life on School Field.*

I mumbled, "What's . . ."

"Read it," Todd said.

I tried to.

> The body of Frain High School All-County pitcher Rudy Beavich was found by a groundskeeper early Sunday morning on the pitcher's mound of the school baseball diamond. Beavich died of a gunshot wound to the left temple, an apparent suicide victim, an Ortega, California, police spokesman said.

I glanced at Todd, but he was reading with me, his lips moving slightly.

> Beavich, one of the most successful athletes in Frain history, was surrounded by several trophies and plaques he had been awarded over the course of a high school career *Ortega Courier* sports editor, Marty Amlin, called "meteoric" in a profile last May.

"The poor guy," Todd said again.

> Detective Frank Cardini refused to speculate as to the significance of the various awards that Beavich had apparently brought with him to the pitcher's mound.
>
> Beavich had given no indication in recent weeks that he was unhappy, friends reported. "He had a great season, and was just looking forward to graduation and the summer," teammate Dave Melchior said.

"Listen." My eyes were blurry from the strain, and I rubbed them. "I think we should go."

"You know what's funny?" Todd said in a quiet voice. "I can sort of understand it, you know?"

I had to swallow first, and even then I couldn't answer.

"The pressure." He whistled a sigh between his teeth. "The pressure he must have felt."

"Yeah," I agreed, though I'd seen Todd pitch for almost ten years in every kind of situation and never once had he mentioned pressure.

"It's just . . . real sad," he whispered.

"How long," I tried to pose it delicately, "how long have you been looking at that?"

But he didn't hear me. He had gone back to the beginning, reading the whole story through yet another time.

"Sorry, Paulie," Mr. Bannister told me, the next time I stopped by after dinner. "You missed Todd. He's at the library, hitting those books."

"Mr. B." I glanced at his wristwatch. "Doesn't the library close at eight?"

I could see that threw him. "Maybe it does, maybe it does. Well, he'll probably be right home then. You can wait in Todd's room if you like," he offered.

"Okay." I trotted after him up the stairs, thinking maybe I was overdoing it, always worrying about Todd. Why couldn't I be more like his dad? He seemed to—

I lost that thought the moment I stepped into Todd's room and saw the bare walls.

They must be painting, I thought. That had to be why almost all the walls of Todd's room were stripped clean—by the window, where the framed newspaper articles and the plaques had hung; on the wall by his closet, the three shelves that had held his trophies; over his bedboard, where he'd kept the faded ribbons and certificates that went back to Little League.

All gone. And no, it wasn't painting. It was cleaning.

Todd had cleaned away every bit of who he was.

"Mr. B.—how long ago—what's going on with—"

"Oh," he looked past me to the walls. "You mean, where are his trophies, and that? You know, he didn't say this, but I think . . ." He paused, and when he spoke again his voice was a little huskier. "I think they hurt, Paulie. Every day, seeing all . . . what he used to be, and that. And now, with his eye . . ."

I nodded. "I know."

"So I asked him. 'Is that why you took it all down?' " Mr. Bannister brushed at a tear. "He put his arm around me, right here, where we're standing, and he said, 'Don't worry, Dad. Everything's under control.' " He shook his head and sighed. "Can you believe that, Paulie? After all he's been through, there he is, trying to reassure *me*."

I waited in his room till eight-thirty that night, but he didn't get home.

The next time I called it was Sunday. The missing trophies were just the latest on the long list of things I knew I ought to ask about. I never got the chance. His dad answered the phone, and Todd was out.

"Out?" I protested. "Where'd he—"

Mr. B. cut me off. "He, uh, went to see about a job, Paulie."

"A job? On Sunday night?"

His voice stumbled. "It's . . . well, I think it's a weekend job. . . ."

Listen to him, I thought. He doesn't know *where* Todd is. Or where he's been, all these nights.

Of course, neither did I, but I could find out. Monday morning I got to school early and camped out by his locker. When he finally arrived I lit into him. "Where the hell were you last night?"

"Where was I?" He dialed his combination, angling his head a little bit extra to see on his right side. It made it look as if he was turning away, and got me madder.

"Don't play dumb. You weren't looking for any job. Not on Sunday night. Where were you?"

"Is that what my dad said?" He shook his head. "He always gets it wrong. I was over at Steve Bates's last night."

"Steve *Bates?*"

"Yeah."

"You're not," I stammered, "you're not a friend of Steve Bates."

Todd grunted. "He's not such a bad guy."

By then I wasn't even sure what I was accusing him of. Todd waited. "Well," he looked at his watch. "I've got to get to economics. . . ."

I drifted along beside him, still fumbling for words. When the crowd from the stairway emptied into the hall I nodded so long and turned in the opposite direction to get to math. For a moment everyone ahead of me slowed up. I pushed to get by, and then I saw Mrs. Pierman, the social worker, brush past with a freshman girl in tow. While the girl sniffled beside her, she unlocked her office door, murmuring, "It's okay, now, it's okay."

The kids surged on and I went with them, but all at once my knees locked up on me. I took a couple of bumps from behind; I hardly noticed. Against the flow I retraced my steps until I stood a couple of feet outside Mrs. Pierman's office. The heavy door swung shut in my face.

A kid, hustling to beat the bell to his next class, rammed my shoulder, but still I didn't move.

It wasn't Mrs. Pierman I was there for. I was only around her once, a year ago, in the spring. Some senior girl had taken a bunch of pills, and left school to go to a hospital for the rest of the semester. I didn't know the girl, and had barely heard about it before Mrs. Pierman showed up in our English class.

Mrs. Pierman, talking about the warning signs of suicide.

That's why I was staring. I was seeing right through her door, back to that English class, hearing what she had said all over again.

Someone will seem troubled, she had said, *depressed, and then suddenly seem all right. Happy, even, though there's no apparent reason why.*

Don't worry about it, he kept telling me.

That's a dangerous sign. Mrs. Pierman had waited till each one of us in the class returned her gaze before going on. *It means the person has made a decision, and a suicide attempt could be soon.*

I heard Mr. Bannister's shaky voice. What was it Todd said to him?

Everything's under control.

There are other signs to look for, too. There's often the urge to give away possessions. . . .

I pulled off my Cardinals cap and fingered the fine wool around the logo. A twenty-five dollar cap. "You want it?" he had asked, without a second's hesitation.

Now, instead of seeing the dull green of Mrs. Pierman's door, I saw the pale spots on his walls where the awards and certificates had hung.

What would he do next? Hand me an All-County trophy, or maybe a plaque or two? They're no good to me, Paulie. You take them.

Unless he had a better use.

I saw the picture of that boy in California, the kid pitcher from a few years back. I saw his expression in the microfilm photo, the edgy look of someone ready to bolt at any moment.

The kid—and the trophies surrounding him on the pitcher's mound. Probably the last things he ever saw.

And he hadn't even lost an eye.

Todd's words from his first week back at school resounded inside me—*I was alive then. I'm dead now.*

I started nodding to myself, right there in the hall, like a crazy man so convinced he was right he could carry on both parts of a conversation.

Todd, gaping at the article in the library, reading it through again and again.

It all made sense. The worst kind, the kind you didn't see till afterward. Because all your friends and family said, *"Just leave him be. Stop worrying. Let him work it out for himself."*

Just what Rudy Beavich's friends must have said.

And what was I doing all this time? His guardian angel, wasn't that what I had called myself? It sounded nice, but what was I *really* doing? Planning computer tricks with my brother while Todd was off somewhere at night, and not even his parents knew where.

How long before they called me out of some class to find my mom or dad waiting for me in the office with the news?

It means a person has made a decision. . . .

I knew where he had economics. And where he had math. And Spanish, and English, all those rooms—

And I knew I'd be standing outside when the bell went off, waiting to meet him, walk with him, watch over him. I'd fly from one end of the school to the other to be there before him.

Because I had no choice now. There were times even a guardian angel had to land, wings and all, on somebody's back and wrestle him to the ground. I would, too, before I let Todd end up like Rudy Beavich.

Chapter 13

What I should have done was tell my parents, or Todd's parents, or even Mrs. Pierman. Hadn't she advised that? *You can't help someone all by yourself.* But what could I say, and who would believe me? Worse, what would Todd think when it got back to him?

I could tell on him, all right. It would only end our friendship right there.

So that chilly Monday evening I found a hiding place in some shrubbery a few houses down from Todd's, but with a clear view of his front door, and waited. Maybe I'd see nothing. Maybe, by nine or so, I could give up for the night, go home and go to bed. I'd need my rest, after all. There was tomorrow, and the next day, and the next. . . .

About seven-fifteen the porch light at the Bannisters' went on briefly. I squinted, and saw Todd's silhouette coming down the front steps.

The light clicked off, but in the dim glow of the streetlight I could still see him. He turned to the side of the house, back to the garage. Scared already of losing him, I darted to a mailbox and huddled there for cover.

The creak of the Bannisters' garage door cut through the

night. Todd's figure vanished as he ducked inside. I peeked around the side of the mailbox. When he emerged, his shape seemed larger. Bulky. Confused, I stared harder. I heard his footsteps hurrying back down the driveway, and when he reached the street he turned left, the opposite direction from the library. Yeah, some research paper, I thought. At the corner another streetlight illuminated him, and I saw why his shape had changed.

Over his shoulder he lugged a duffel bag. It was heavy enough so that he trudged along a little top-heavy, his feet moving briskly to match his momentum.

He crossed the street and was almost half a block away before I could spring from the mailbox and follow him. At first I sprinted from tree to telephone pole to parked car for cover. But the more I thought about the duffel bag, the more my heart pounded impatiently, and soon I was jogging after him without a thought of concealing myself.

The air was cold and thin. I could have trailed him by the scuffing sound of his footsteps alone. After a couple more blocks he paused at a busy street. I crouched by somebody's front steps. He crossed over. And then I knew.

He was heading for the park.

When he disappeared into the shadows under the stone arch at the entrance, I gulped down a breath and hurried after him. I was desperate to keep up, and scared, and furious with myself for not telling anyone. Now was it too late? Could I afford to leave him while I hunted for a phone, or ran back to his house?

The park was supposed to close at dusk, but all you got on

winter evenings were a few nutty joggers. Who was there to notice Todd and his bundle? I crossed the street, scampered through the arch. Twenty yards farther, the path divided into three, and I stood, panting, wondering which way he had gone.

Which way? I sneered to myself. I knew which way, and what he was doing, too.

I tried to imagine the look on his face as I hurried to the ballfield—was it that eerie cheerfulness, or something stonier, his good eye fixed straight ahead?

There were lights along the paths, and one security floodlight behind the backstop. A faint glow spilled over the diamond. When I finally spied him, near the fence along right field, I heard a quiet whimper escape my lips. When he slipped through the opening in the fence, I knew I was done waiting. I left the shadows and raced down the hill to the field.

Todd had reached the pitcher's mound. His figure bobbed in front of me as my feet stumbled across the uneven ground. Kneeling down, he groped in the bag.

I vaulted the fence like a hurdles champ, almost flying across the infield. At the last second he heard the sound of my approach and spun toward me. I lunged and seized an arm, but he was all adrenaline from the sudden fright; he dipped his shoulder and flicked me past him.

I landed hard on the mound and scrambled to my feet. "What are you doing here?" I screamed at him.

"What are *you* doing here? You scared the hell out of me."

I hunkered down, ready to barrel into him again if I had to. "What's in the bag?" I gasped for breath.

He tried to scoot it behind him with his foot. "What do you care?"

"You think you're going to be like that kid in California, don't you?"

"What kid?"

"You know—the one who—"

"What are you *talking* about?"

His body uncoiled for just a second, and I leaped for him, throwing my shoulder into his knees. I tried to free the bag from under us, but he caught it, yanked it away, and shoved me off.

"*What the hell is wrong with you?*" he cried. He saw me staring wide-eyed, glanced down at the bag, and then back at me. "God, Paulie. Now I get it." He nodded. "The kid from California . . ."

"What's in the bag?" I said, alert for the best chance to pounce again.

His angry face cracked into a grin. "You want to know what's in here?" He shook his head and smiled sickly, as if just catching on he'd been the butt of someone's bad joke. "You really want to know?"

I nodded, carefully.

He overturned the bag, and out tumbled a pile of garage-sale junk: twisted coat hangers, yardsticks, cardboard tubes, wooden slats, some duct tape, a couple of gloves, a pair of hard plastic goggles, and a dozen smudged-up baseballs.

My eyes flitted everywhere. No trophies, no plaques, and certainly no gun. Nothing he could hurt himself with. I felt my muscles go slack.

"There," Todd shouted. "How's that?" He tossed the empty bag aside, still shaking his head.

"Listen, I'm sorry, I—" I kneeled down and sorted through the pile, too bewildered to be ashamed. "What is this stuff?"

"You want to see?" Todd stooped by the odd pile of sticks and wire and began assembling something. First he taped the yardsticks together into a tripod. On top of that he arranged the cardboard tubes to form a rectangle, the long sides vertical, and reinforced it with the wooden slats. He secured it with more tape, his tongue out the side of his mouth in concentration. From the top crossbar of the rectangle he rigged a coat hanger and hung a beat-up old catcher's mitt. When he finally stepped back, the whole contraption resembled some spindly three-legged alien who had wandered onto the ballfield by mistake. Todd carefully picked it up. I followed him to the backstop, where, in the weak light, he placed it directly behind home plate.

Gauging its position for a second, he turned to me. "You ever hear of Herb Score?"

"Herb Score," I murmured. The name was familiar.

"He pitched for the Indians back in the fifties. Unbelievable fastball. Superstar potential. Then"—he clapped his hands together—"*bang.*"

"He got hit," I said suddenly, "in the eye." *Herb Score.* I *knew* I had heard of him. "He got hit," my voice trailed off, "by a line drive."

"That book you gave me a couple of years ago, *Heroes of the American League?* He was in there. Could have been one of the greatest pitchers ever, then blind in one eye at twenty-three." Todd bit his lip, glancing around as if to be sure no one was listening. "You know what happened?"

I shook my head.

"He came back. Everybody said, 'Give it up, Herb.' But he fought his way back and pitched five more years in the big leagues." He stared at me as I'd never seen him stare down a batter. "What about it, Mr. Baseball Historian? You're the guy who knows every batting average, and ERA, and who won every World Series. How come you didn't once mention Herb Score to me?"

He caught me stealing a look at the rickety thing astride home plate. "You figure out what that is yet?"

I took a step toward it. The shorter, horizontal sticks covered just the width of the plate. The vertical sides spanned just about from my armpits to my knees.

"It's a strike zone." I turned quickly to face him. "You've been working out." He nodded. "Here, at night. You haven't been at the library at all."

"Just that night you ran into me."

"Why didn't you tell me?"

Todd looked away, over my head, and swallowed. "You know how hard it is to even say it? *I still think I can pitch.*" A wisp of frozen breath escaped him. "There. That was the first time. Out loud, anyway."

I held out my hands, pleading my innocence. "How was I supposed to—"

"You could have *asked,*" Todd roared. "You are my goddamn best friend. For four months you haven't even *mentioned* baseball to me. Why the hell didn't you just—I don't know—ask me if I was going to pitch."

"I guess . . . I was afraid."

"Afraid? Of what?"

"I don't know," I mumbled. But I did.

I was afraid he'd say yes.

"I knew, ever since that party, the one I threw up all over myself—I knew I was going to try."

The strike zone target stood beside us, the catcher's mitt dangling in the faint breeze. I pointed to it. "How long have you been using this?"

Todd shrugged. "About three weeks."

"Your poor dad, all this time—"

"Don't you think he knew?" Todd asked. "We never said much about it, but he knew where I was going. He would have driven me if I wanted. Waited for me. But he knew I had to do this alone."

"It didn't have to be alone," I said. "We could have met after school." Now I was the resentful one. "We could have used the gym, instead of you sneaking around—"

"No." He wasn't about to be scolded. "What do you think, I wanted everybody to feel *sorry* for me? Poor Todd, he used to be somebody, now he's got to start all over being a *nobody.* How do you think that would feel?"

"I don't know," I said softly. "I was always a nobody."

He ignored that, just said, low and quickly, "I'm going to do it."

I thought of the missing trophies, the article on the microfilm—all the clues that had propped up my greatest fear.

"How come you took down the stuff in your room?" I said.

He frowned. "You really don't get it, do you, Paulie? That guy in the photos. That's not me anymore."

"Sure it is."

"*It isn't,*" he said. "Not anymore. I don't *feel* like him." He smiled dourly, and I saw the dull glint of lamplight on his plastic eye. "I don't *look* like him. And I don't need him watching over me, judging how I'm doing."

"But how come you've been so *happy* lately?"

"Happy?"

"Like with that message to Melissa I had Tyler send. You just laughed about it. I haven't seen you like that in months."

He thought about it. "You want to know why?" He plucked a baseball from the ground and pointed with it toward the strike-zone structure. "Because last week for the first time I threw *three goddamn strikes in a row,* that's why." He smiled, recalling. "Right through the zone. With a little heat on them, too. You know how hard it is to get something over the plate when everything looks so flat to me with just one eye? *You know how stupid I feel sometimes out here?*"

He didn't wait for me to answer; he gathered half a dozen balls and backtracked to the mound. I stayed there, halfway to first, and watched. He peeled off his jacket and stretched for a while, jogged from the mound to second and back a couple times. He carefully drew the goggles down over his eyes, tugged at the strap, then lobbed a few balls lightly, not even aiming for the plate. I was invisible to him now; it could have been any night the past three weeks. In a minute he went to fetch those balls and scooped up the rest, returning to the mound. Soon he was limbered up, and throwing from a full windup. The first pitch was low, knocking over the yardstick legs and upending the target. Todd strode purposely toward it, exhaling through his teeth as if he'd done this a thousand times, and set the contraption upright again. He steadied himself on the mound, peered in as if for a sign, went through his windup, and hurled another pitch toward the plate.

It nicked the right side, spinning the rectangle around and then down to the ground.

Again he started toward it, and that's when I beat him to the thing, lying cockeyed in the dirt. I yelled, "This is stupid," ripped the catcher's mitt free, and held up the strike-zone target so he could see it from the edge of the mound. "Look at this." I shook it in contempt. "It's just stupid," I said again, and tossed it away.

"Hey, leave it," Todd yelled.

I slipped the mitt onto my left hand, kicked at the frozen dirt behind the plate, and crouched down. "Just pitch," I snapped. I mumbled to myself, making certain he could hear me, "Of all the dumb . . . ridiculous . . . *stupid* ideas. . . ."

"Fastballs first," Todd called. "Okay?"

"*Just throw the ball.*" The first pitch was high; I had to spring up to snare it. "Nice," I snorted. "I'm really impressed." I flung the ball back to him and looked away. I was grinning so broadly I felt my eyes start to water, but I wasn't going to let him see it.

136

Not yet, anyway.

The next pitch was closer to the strike zone. "Follow through," I shouted.

Then another, closer still. Maybe even a strike. I kept ranking on Todd, between pitches, sometimes gesturing to the pile of wood and wire off to my left and shaking my head in exaggerated scorn. And soon more of his pitches than not passed for strikes, and once or twice from the worn old mitt I heard the sweet pop of his fastball, and soon I wasn't saying anything, and neither was Todd. By then I didn't care who saw me smiling. I knew what was right, what was best for Todd, even as the next pitch bounced two feet before home plate and caromed off my hip.

To hell with what I'd been trying all winter, to pamper and protect him. To hell, even, with Melissa. If Todd could believe, then I sure as hell could, too. Because this, I saw, was the way back for him, it always had been: on a little hill of dirt sixty feet from his best friend.

Part Three
CONTROL

Chapter 14

I first spotted the signs on a Monday, posted all around the school. MANDATORY VARSITY BASEBALL MEETING, WED., 3 O'CLOCK. For the next two days my life was nothing but a prolonged countdown to that meeting. I was the first one there, of course, and while I waited for Todd to show up I tried to look nonchalant, flexing the old worn catcher's glove I'd been using at our workouts.

"Hey, it's Lockwood," Harley Shawn sneered when he saw me. Harley was probably the second-best pitcher on the team, after Todd. He had a pretty good fastball, but what he really had was attitude. He'd bark at his infielders, complain to the ump for every pitch that wasn't a strike. He always wore his baseball cap, on the field or in the halls at school, pulled down so low if you tried to look him in the eye all you'd see was brim. "Don't tell me you're a catcher now."

I should have ignored him, but I heard myself mumble, "Maybe backup. Thought I'd try it."

"Hey, Bates, hear that?" Harley called across the room. "Meet the new catcher." He glanced around to see how much of an audience he had. "Infielder. Outfielder. Catcher. Lockwood, where the hell *haven't* you played?" And then before anyone could answer, he said, "Oh, right, the first six innings, that's where."

Even Coach Benedict, sitting up front, couldn't help grinning. I tried to fix a hearty Mr. Good Sport look on my face.

The moment Todd walked through the door all the chuckling stopped.

He nodded to Coach Benedict and some of the other guys, and took a seat beside me. I would have paid ten bucks to see the way Harley's jaw dropped, so it was even better free: He tilted back the bill of his cap and looked as dazed as a mole caught in the sunlight. Even after Benedict started the meeting, Harley kept glancing back at Todd, as if he still couldn't believe he was there.

Take that, Harley, I thought. Todd Bannister's back, and Paulie Roy Lockwood's with him.

The first real practice was the next day in the gym. Todd and I stood watching Harley air out his practice tosses. From the moment he walked into the gym, it wasn't just Harley Getting Loose, but the Showboat Express: exaggerated windup, a hearty grunt with every pitch, and several seconds to shake out his arm and strut around. To me it all spelled *Memo from Harley to Todd: Meet the new ace.*

"What a jerk," I said to Todd.

He didn't answer, only folded his arms, studying Harley.

"As long as you're around," I continued, "Harley'll never be more than—"

Just then Rishi Patel and Luther Henderson emerged from the locker-room door, almost bumping into us. Like everyone

142

else in the school these days, they stopped and stared at Todd's right eye.

"It looks great, hey?" Luther said, grinning. "Rishi, don't that look great?"

Rishi agreed. I thought by this time Todd might be getting fed up with all the attention his new prosthesis was getting, but he just nodded appreciatively. It was only a week since he'd gone to New York City with his mother to sit for the specialist—a guy whose job it was to hand paint a prosthesis so it matched your good eye. Luther was right, it *was* a great job. If you looked close you could even see little blood vessels painted in. Sometimes the eye seemed to have a luster to it, as if it were really a part of him, and not just plastic. More people had stopped and looked him squarely in the face in the last week than had even *mentioned* the eye in the last five months.

Luther pointed to the goggles dangling from Todd's neck. "And you're gonna wear those things, right?"

Todd slipped them on. "That's right." He smiled. "Don't want to mess up a work of art."

Then Coach Z—I hadn't seen him since Todd was in the hospital—shuffled over. He greeted us all, then turned to Todd. "How are you, boy?" He reached out and cupped his shoulder affectionately.

"Z, check out those goggles." Luther grinned. "The man's making a fashion statement."

Coach Z leaned back, appraising. Now, I thought, we'll hear about the old days, how they never had that kind of stuff in the old days. . . .

But all he said was, "Are you sure"—he licked his lips—"are you sure this is the right thing, Todd?"

"The right thing?" I murmured to myself.

"I'm sure, Coach," Todd said, holding his gaze.

"Your doctor says it's all right?"

Todd tapped one of the oversized lenses. "As long as I wear these."

"And what about your mom and dad?"

"It's okay with them." Coach Z just watched him. Todd shrugged nervously. "Really, it is."

"You don't have any trouble, somebody throws you the ball?"

Jeez, Coach, I thought. Come *on*.

"Huh-uh. No trouble at all." Todd told him how we'd been working out. I could almost see the thoughts churning furiously behind Coach Z's lumpy, nicked-up face.

"How about up at bat? You tried taking any pitches?"

"No, not yet." Todd was getting a little impatient. Just let him *play*, I wanted to say. He probably would have kept Todd there all afternoon, asking about stuff nobody else in the world would have thought of, if Benedict hadn't blown his whistle from the other end of the gym for the team to assemble.

Coach Z nodded, tight-lipped. "You're a hell of a kid," he finally said. "It's going to be tough."

"I know," Todd said.

Not half as tough as *talking* about it, I thought.

"Man," Luther Henderson cooed in admiration. I think we were all relieved to turn his way and find him still ogling Todd's prosthesis. "It looks *perfect*," he said, and we laughed. Then he asked, without even disguising the wonder, "And you're gonna get up there and *pitch*, right?"

Todd allowed a tight smile. "That's right."

"Damn." Luther shook his head. "Damn."

"You should have seen him," I said a few nights later at dinner. "As soon as he started throwing, you could tell."

"You think he'll be able to play?" my mom asked.

"Play?" I gobbled down a mouthful. "Mom—he's going to be *Todd*."

"And those goggles are working out all right?" my dad asked.

"No problem," I crowed. "After a while you don't even notice them. Control's still a little off, but velocity's great." I thought back to the workout that afternoon. It was the first day Benedict had had batters stand in against the pitchers. The pitchers weren't supposed to burn it in one hundred percent yet, especially not this year, when the pitching was a little thin anyway. After Todd and Harley, there was Spiros Demopoulos, who was a better violinist than a pitcher—he was First Chair for the County Youth Orchestra. Then Steve Bates, if you wanted to count him; he was always nagging Benedict to let him pitch. After those four, there was nobody, so Benedict was babying them, not wanting any sore arms. Even so, Todd's pitches at half speed were still a blur to most batters. I couldn't help but snicker at Frankie Flynn, poised at the plate with a bat. When a couple of Todd's throws got away from him, poor Frankie went diving for cover like somebody caught out in an air raid. After that Frankie could hardly swing, even when some of the pitches were right over the plate.

"Well, that's wonderful," Mom said. She turned to Dad. "I wonder if he'll be able to play in college."

"College?" I put down my fork. "Of *course* he'll be able to play in college—if he goes."

"If he goes?" Dad asked. Oops. Wrong thing to say. Dad had been more and more antsy lately about college; the SATs were only eight weeks away. I was so sick of his threatening (oh, I'm sorry, I mean *encouraging*) me to take them that I had finally registered just so he would leave me alone. Except he didn't. Now he was drilling me on analogies at dinner every night. Thank God, for the moment, we were talking about Todd.

"What I'm saying," I sighed—you wouldn't think it would be so hard to get something across to people as smart as my folks—"is he may not *have* to go to college now. Not once people see how he can throw."

"You're talking about the majors." Dad phrased it delicately. "You still think they're interested?"

"They will be," I said, "if he keeps pitching like this."

Mom cupped her chin in her palms. "It's almost too much to hope for."

"Well, just wait." I smiled. "Just watch us."

Of course all Tyler could do was glance over and chirp, "*Us?*"

After the first week of practice Todd wanted to keep working out in the park on our own, so we met a few evenings each week and on Saturdays. Sometimes we'd just run, or I'd bunt balls to his left and right to see how fast he could get off the mound and field them. But pitching was why we were there. He threw for at least twenty minutes, every other day.

One evening we were packing up to go when I noticed Todd hadn't even pulled off his spikes. He slouched forward on the bench, looking out over the field.

"You going to stay here all night?" I said.

"Paulie." He frowned in thought. "Can you grab a bat while I throw some more? Don't swing, just stand in the batter's box."

"Is this about today?" I asked. That afternoon, at practice, a couple of guys had hit some shots off Todd—line drives I'd rarely seen him give up.

He nodded. "I just can't get comfortable with a guy at bat. I'm . . . I'm afraid I'll hit him."

"Hey," I scoffed. "Who cares about the batter? That's why they're getting hits off you. You're just aiming the ball over the plate. You're not letting loose."

"I'm a little worried about my control," Todd said. "The curve's even worse. I don't know where that's going."

I grabbed a bat, took a few swings and stood at the plate. "Just throw," I called to him. "Stop thinking. Let 'er rip."

He tossed a few warm-ups. "Now crouch," he said. "Crowd the plate a little." He hummed five or six fastballs waist high. They looked pretty good to me.

"Now I'm going with the curve," he yelled from the mound.

I remembered back in middle school how Todd always got me to drop the bat and duck for shelter while his curve broke perfectly over the plate. Sure enough, the first one he snapped off headed right for me. I waited. Hang in there, I thought. It'll break away from you—

"Ow," I yelled. The ball plunked me in the side.

"Sorry."

"No problem," I called to him. "Didn't even hurt."

But the next one sure did—"*Ee-yow!*"—drilling me in the elbow. Over the next three or four pitches, one nicked me in the shoulder, another got my thigh.

"Go back to the fastball," I said. "This time, just burn it."

He did; a little high, it shot past me and rattled the backstop.

"That's the way." I cocked the bat back. "That's how you—"

I never finished. The next pitch came straight for my head. Somehow I scrambled out of the box as the ball roared by.

"Hey," I whimpered, picking myself off the ground.

Todd shook his head. "See? There's something wrong."

"Yeah," I joked. "I'm not wearing armor."

He didn't come close to a smile.

Two evenings later, trudging down the hill toward the field, I stopped and stared.

At first it looked as if parts of Todd were scattered all over the diamond, as if a pack of dogs had gotten hold of a scarecrow. His glove was lying out past second base. A crumpled sweatshirt was in a heap at home plate. Finally I spotted Todd, five feet from the backstop, firing ball after ball into the old screen. The rusty wire shrieked in protest.

148

I trotted up to him uneasily. "I thought we said six-thirty. Sorry I'm late—"

He turned, not a bit surprised at my voice. "You're not late." His dark eyebrows met in one long ridge of anger.

"What's wrong?"

"What's wrong? Roll up your sleeve. Your left one."

"What?"

"Go on."

I squinted at him for a second, then slipped out of my windbreaker and pushed up the sleeve.

Todd pointed to two purplish yellow spots around my elbow. "What are those?"

"What do they look like?" I said. "They're bruises."

"Where'd you get them?"

I scrunched down my sleeve. "I got them from you. You know that. What's the big deal? Think I can't take a pitch or two?"

"The big deal is, it's not working out." He knelt down, gathering the loose balls and dropping them into his duffel bag. "Let's go home. Let's forget about it."

"*Forget* about it?" I didn't stoop to help him. "What do you mean?"

He sat down on the ground, drew his legs up to his chest. "I think . . . maybe this whole idea was stupid."

He looked up quickly, watching me, as if all I had to do was nod my head a fraction of an inch and he'd pack up and never come back.

Instead I said, with as much of an edge as I could muster,

"Stupid?" He wasn't ready for that. "What's *stupid* is coming this far and quitting."

"Come on, Paulie. Face it. I'm not the pitcher I was. I'm not even average, now."

"Average?" Suddenly I was yelling. "I can't believe you. You've got all this talent. And all these people pulling for you. You've got everything."

"Don't forget the plastic eye," he mumbled.

"Yeah, and you know what? Since you got it painted it looks great, okay? You ever look in the mirror?"

"Yeah." Todd climbed slowly to his feet. "I do. I see this guy in the mirror. And he looks fine. If I don't lean over the sink too closely, if I don't get right up into his face—I wouldn't know anything had ever happened to him." He chewed his lip. "But me . . . the guy who's looking *at* the guy in the mirror. I'm still looking out of one eye. It's still all—closed in and narrow and flat. And you know what, Paulie?" His voice flared up. "I'm *jealous* of that guy in the mirror. 'Cause I'm not him."

I turned away from him, glanced around the diamond. I saw the two of us for the last five weeks freezing our butts off out here, working out. I remembered how pleased I was, helping him come back. How good it made me feel.

It's still not enough, I thought.

"Look," I said, and once again I shoved up the sleeve of my sweatshirt. I pinched a bruise between my forefinger and thumb. "Pretty ugly, isn't it?"

"Definitely ugly." I almost thought he smiled.

"You know why?"

He nodded, sad again. "Because I can't find the plate—"

150

"Because," I interrupted, "your *goddamn arm* is still a million-dollar arm. Good eye or not. Fastball or curve. You think these are *high school* bruises?"

He grinned sheepishly. "I don't know."

"This is a *major league* bruise, pal. It's a *Todd Bannister* bruise."

"Get out of here," he reddened.

I didn't grin back. "You can't quit, you hear me? You haven't given one hundred percent yet. And one hundred percent is hauling back and smoking the ball home and not worrying about the *batter,* or the *ump,* and especially not about some guy in the *mirror.*" I flipped him a ball. "Let's get warmed up. I didn't come all this way for nothing."

"Here." I handed the two sheets of computer paper to Melissa. "We're even now."

"Even?" she mumbled, a pencil in her mouth, her glasses perched on her brow. "Even for what?"

"For . . . ," I shuffled my feet, "you know. That day in the computer room."

Her eyes narrowed with the beady expression of a sniper. "You really think you could make up for that with *one article. . . .*"

"You said I could."

"I was being kind. One article's a start." She went back to scanning the mock-up of the front page in despair.

I said, "Aren't you going to read it?"

She murmured, distracted, "Sure. Of course."

"So read it now." I tried to slip the story under her gaze. "Come on, Melissa, you'll like it."

She tossed off a dramatic sigh and gathered up the article. I watched everything—how her brow tightened, her eyes squinted, her mouth pursed to a thoughtful *O*. About the third paragraph in she started chewing on a nail and wouldn't let it go.

At last she looked up.

"Paulie. You're sure about this?" Her tone was suspicious, but in her eyes there was nothing but hope.

"Of course I am." I peered over her shoulder and we mouthed the headline together.

Todd Bannister to Pitch First Game of Season.

"How do you know this?" She jumped on me suddenly. "How come there aren't more quotes?"

"I—"

"Who'd you interview? Where are your *sources?*"

"They're . . . they're confidential, that's what. I've got to protect them."

"Paulie. This isn't Washington, D.C. Who are you protecting them *from?*"

"From . . ." I could feel myself faltering, and then it came to me. "From *Benedict,* Melissa. See, nobody's supposed to know this yet."

"But—why—"

"If you were an athlete you'd understand." I pointed to the article. "It's a scoop, is what it is."

She looked up, beyond the paper, then back again. And when she finally spoke she didn't sound any more like an editor than I did. She sounded like a friend. "He's really going to pitch? He's really—he can do it?"

"Melissa." I could hear my own excitement. "I've been watching him. Working out with him. I *know*. Lots of guys get injured. The guys like Todd—the guys with as much heart as he's got—they come back."

She turned away, pressed at her eyelids with a thumb and forefinger. I kept on.

"You don't need quotes for that," I said. "Right now . . . you've just got to believe."

She cleared her throat. "It's a wonderful story. Not just for the paper. For . . . well, for Todd." She looked at me. "He must be . . . so happy."

A month ago I would have said *Why don't you ask him yourself?*

This time I wasn't getting distracted.

"So—you're going to use it?"

"I'd rather have some more—you really ought to—" She shut her eyes and shook her head. Then she shivered, those long lashes bobbed up, and she met my gaze. "Oh, hell." Her smile glimmered naughtily. "Let's do it."

Chapter 15

I didn't get any abuse when *Bannister to Pitch First Game of Season* came out in *Panther Paws*. I didn't hear a thing. It was as if the whole school had gasped and held its breath. You couldn't miss the article: Melissa used large bold type for the headline, and copies were strewn all over the cafeteria, in the classrooms, in the halls.

For most of that morning I had managed to avoid Todd, but just after fourth period, stowing my books in my locker before gym, I felt him reach out and snag my collar. "What," he held the sports page up to my nose, "is this?"

I stammered through my explanation of how *nothing* in the article *wasn't* true, if you *thought* about it, how Benedict *had* to start him, what *choice* did he have, there was no reason to get all *steamed* about it, and . . .

And then I saw a smile struggling to escape him. I slumped with relief. He gritted his teeth to stay stern. "Okay, what about this part?" He read from the article, " *'You can sure tell Todd's been working out all winter,* a member of the team said.' " He looked up. "A member of the team. That's you, Paulie, isn't it?"

"Well, it's true. I can tell."

"I can't believe the only person you interviewed is yourself. You didn't even interview *me*."

"I didn't have to," I said. "I'm your best friend. I *knew* what you'd say."

He made a big show of looking annoyed. "Well, next time—"

"Look at you," I teased. "You're *smiling*. You're glad I wrote it, aren't you?"

Todd glanced around. "That's not what I'm smiling about," he said. "Somebody called me last night," he grinned.

I shook my head, not catching on, until the answer burst in front of me. "A *scout*," I rasped. "An *agent*."

"Well, no." Then he beamed, "But a sportswriter. From Albany. He wanted to know when I'd be pitching."

"So what'd you tell him?"

"What do you think?" He headed toward his class with a grin. "I told him to ask you."

"Don't you get it?" I scolded Melissa. "A *sportswriter*? From *Albany?*"

"Uh-huh," she agreed. "That's great."

"Of *course* it's great. Today Albany, tomorrow New York City. . . ."

"Sure."

"And after that—*Melissa*," I shouted. "You don't even act *surprised*."

"Why should I?" She started to giggle, right in my face.

"Why *should* you? You know what it means? It means they're *interested* in him again. It means—wait a minute."

She watched with total delight as I figured it out.

"It's because of you, isn't it?" I accused.

"Now don't go making a big thing out of—"

"The sportswriter. You called him. And you told—"

"I told him about Todd. About his pitching again."

"How?" I stammered. "Who? . . ."

She tried to shrug it off. "He was a writer I met last summer, when I did that internship there. He said to call him if I ever had a story. So I did."

"Yeah, but . . ." I rubbed my brow. "You did that—just to help Todd?"

"I just made a phone call, that's all—" Her eyes grew suspicious. "Paulie—you're not going to tell Todd?"

"*No,*" I blurted obediently, as if she might take it all back with a wave of her hand. "But . . . why?"

"Just to help him, that's why. And you know what? At first I didn't know if I should, and now—now you tell me how excited he was when he heard from this guy."

"He was. You should have seen him."

"Well, now I'm glad I did. I feel good about it."

"I know," I nodded, smiling. "I know just what you mean."

Besides Todd and Melissa and my mom and dad (you'd think I wrote the Declaration of Independence the way they walked around the house, reading the article out loud), hardly anybody else even mentioned the story to me.

Except, of course, Coach Benedict.

He didn't say anything directly. He didn't have to. By now we were practicing outdoors at the park, and there were endless ways he could let me know what he thought about my journalistic talent. He had me rake the infield down before and after practice. He had me track down every foul ball no matter where it landed, throw batting practice till my arm felt ready to fall off. (Once, just kidding around, I threw my knurve, and it earned me another set of wind sprints.)

But he never said anything, except one day when he had me fielding bad hops at second and I jammed a finger.

"What's the matter, Lockwood," he called, when he saw me yanking painfully at a knuckle, "afraid you hurt your typing hand?"

I tried to keep out of his way, but by then I wasn't letting Benedict or anybody else slow me down. When Todd was on the mound I'd sneak up behind him and whisper, "Don't hold back," or "Rip it now, *rip* it," or sometimes just, "One hundred percent, okay?"

The first few times he turned, annoyed. But I could see it working. I began to hear the explosive grunt I used to hear when he was really bringing it. He was still wild, but now he wasn't giving in and serving up some wimpy pitch as if that was the only way to get it over the plate. Soon the guys up at bat were stepping back a little, swinging in self-defense. And though he wasn't always throwing strikes, he was giving them something to think about—like wishing they could get out of the batter's box and let somebody else risk his life in there.

Todd, of course, still wasn't satisfied. "Hey, the control will come," I assured him. "Right now you've just got to show who's boss."

✦   ✦   ✦

The next night I was dialing through the static on the old shortwave radio next to my bed. Long ago my dad used it to tune in the world market reports; now that he was online he didn't need it, and gave it to me. If I was lucky, I could pick up games from all over the country. I passed the familiar drone of crowd noise, went back to it and tuned in a game. That was when Tyler came in. He flopped on my bed and said, "That story you wrote. It was super."

I looked over at him, suddenly wary.

"You know," he said, "next time you've got an article to write, you can always use *my* computer. . . ."

"Tyler." I lowered the volume on the game. "What do you want?"

He glanced around nervously, as if he were shoplifting. "Paulie, listen. You owe me a favor."

"For what?"

"That favor I did for you. You know, in the computer room." I squawked in protest. "Okay, so I screwed it up a little. Still, I did it, and you said you'd do something for me, and now I need it. I am your brother, after all."

"How come you only talk about being my brother," I asked, "when you need something?"

Tyler sputtered for a moment, recharging.

"I need to get out of honors English."

For a second I thought I hadn't heard him right. "What's wrong with being in honors English?"

"What's wrong?" His face wrinkled with contempt. "I get *B's*. If I wasn't in honors I'd get *A's*." He twisted around, as if it were so simple there had to be *somebody* in the room who could understand. "It's ruining my future."

"I don't get it—"

"Of course you don't, Paulie. Grades aren't that important to you. But the difference for me between an A or a B is . . . is the difference between getting into the right college."

"Tyler, you're a *freshman*. What do you care about college?"

"Oh, I'm sorry, I should be like you and not care at all."

"I never said that."

"How come you always change the subject when Dad brings it up? How come you don't want to take the SATs?"

"I'm taking them, okay? Just lay off."

"Paulie, listen. The honors class is *harder*. Maybe I'd rather just sit back and *know* I can get an A without having a nervous breakdown trying."

"All right, all right." I sat up. "What do you want me to do?"

"You go to my guidance counselor," Tyler said carefully, "and tell him you wrote all my papers for me. Tell him"—he rolled his eyes upward for inspiration—"tell him I paid you or something, but your conscience finally got the better of you, and you had to tell *somebody*."

"He'll never believe me."

"Why *not?*" Tyler's voice cracked. Great. I couldn't even win an argument with a guy in puberty. "You wrote all those newspaper things."

"Two," I said. "And they're *articles*."

"Tell him you just wanted to help out your little brother, but what's right is right, and I should really be transferred out of honors. . . ."

"But won't he go to Mom and Dad? He'll have to tell them. They'll know I didn't write you any papers."

"I know but . . . I'll figure out something with Mom and Dad. All you need to do"—he sat up, in love with the idea more than ever—"is plant the seed of doubt, okay?"

"And you're going to outwit Mom and Dad and your counselor and your English teacher, right? Forget it," I scoffed. "It'll never work. These are *people* you're talking about, Tyler, not some *computer game.* And people don't always do what you want them to."

"Paulie," he whispered. "Please. Help me. Don't make me read Charles Dickens again."

"Sorry," I said. I cranked up the volume on the radio, and to the grave tones of the announcer describing a three-and-two pitch, I looked Tyler in the eye. "I'm too busy. I'm helping Todd, you understand? I don't have *time* for your little scheme." I watched him, his legs dangling from the bed, his feet not even touching the floor. With a few words, I had made him a freshman again. "We're talking about something a lot bigger here."

Then I turned my back on him to fine-tune the station. Cleveland and Kansas City. Sixth inning. The pitching coach trudged to the mound.

I heard Tyler close the door to my room.

It was no great game, but I listened intently. The Indians were on their fourth pitcher and Kansas City their third. "Another call to the bull pen," the announcer snorted in disgust. "Aren't there any pitchers *anywhere?*"

"I've got one for you," I said. "You just wait."

Chapter 16

When the ball ricocheted off the batting helmet with a sharp screech of plastic, we all froze where we stood, watching the ball arc twenty feet through the air. Only when it came down did we seem to pull our eyes away from it and toward the batter's box, where Rishi Patel lay in the dust, not moving.

In seconds a couple of guys were at his side. Before I joined them I glanced at Todd. He came off the mound in fearful, tentative steps, like an old person confronted with steep stairs. His face was old then, too, a sickly gray.

But when I turned toward Rishi, he was already climbing to his feet. Benedict and Coach Z were there, and Tommy Ricco with an arm around him helped Rishi to the bench. I could hear him say, "I'm okay," hoarsely.

They eased the helmet off him, and only when Bates teased, "Hey, see if there's a dent," and Rishi laughed in reply did I feel myself start breathing again. Now all the guys were joking, nervously at first, then louder.

Except Todd. Standing unsteadily beside me, he croaked, "I'm sorry, Rishi." Nobody heard but me.

Benedict told Rishi he would drive him over to the hospital, just for a precaution. Rishi groaned, "No, I'm all right, I'm all right," but with Austin Wolfe at his side, he followed Benedict to his car.

Coach Z laid a hand on Todd's shoulder as he passed, then rounded everybody up for fungo drills to a roar of complaints.

Todd whispered, "The hospital. He's taking him to the hospital."

"Benedict's just playing it safe," I said. "He—"

Todd was blinking rapidly; his lips were white. For a second I thought he might faint, and I grabbed his arm.

"Hey, come on, shake it off."

"Shake it off? You saw what happened."

"Sure." Coach Z was hollering for me to get out there and play cutoff man. "You hit a batter."

"I hit him in the *head*."

"Okay. Right," I said. "But it wasn't too bad. That's what helmets are for."

Todd mumbled, "I could have killed him."

"Cut it out. You saw him. He was *laughing* about it." I took a step toward Coach Z and the guys in the outfield. "Come *on*," I said. "You've hit a batter before."

Todd shook his head. "Only when I wanted to."

After that it was as if Todd had lost his right arm, too, not just his eye. The fastball was gone. Oh, he still threw a fastball—something without much movement that guys didn't have much trouble hitting. But that big pitch, the million-dollar heater that since the accident had sometimes got away from him and scared hitters all the more because it did—Todd stowed that away like a bad memory.

162

So he didn't start the first game. Harley Shawn did, and pitched well. We won, 5–1. I remember some guy with a notebook and a camera pacing around the stands, a frustrated look on his face. The reporter, I finally realized. The one Melissa had called. No wonder he looked frustrated, driving up from Albany to find Todd nowhere near the mound.

Todd didn't start the next game, either, or even play in the late innings. What was even weirder, I did.

It was late in the second game, when Spiros Demopoulos had to leave for his music lesson. That wasn't as odd as it sounded. By now nobody looked twice when his father stood along the foul line cradling Spiros's violin case, motioning to his watch. Once last year Benedict had tried to pitch him on less than four days rest. From the jayvee game one diamond over I could hear Mr. Demopoulos howl, "He is a *concert violinist,* you know." Now, with Spiros leaving a five-run lead, I thought for sure Benedict would call on Todd. He *had* to. But Benedict ran his eyes quickly down the bench and told Steve Bates to warm up, he was taking over next inning.

I turned to catch Todd's reaction. It was like watching an iguana at the zoo—he didn't even breathe.

"Lockwood," Benedict said. "Start stretching. You're in at second."

I gulped, grabbed my glove, and had the worst case of hiccups in my life.

"Relax," I heard Todd whisper beside me. "You'll do fine."

I didn't. I made an error on one of the first balls hit to me. After that I settled down, though it hardly mattered. Bates got pummeled the moment he took the mound. We lost our lead immediately, and in no time were four runs down. In between batters I checked out Benedict, a few spots down from where Todd huddled on the bench. He hollered encouragement to Bates. When another run scored he rose and started to pace back and forth, right in front of where Todd was sitting—and never once looked at him. That's when it hit me. That there was more to Benedict not playing Todd than how wild he'd been. That what really mattered was putting Todd in his place. He never did like him, after all, ever since Todd stood up to him over those cigarettes. Now he could teach Todd a lesson. I could almost hear him say it. *How's it feel to be just ordinary, big man?*

I ground my fist into my glove. How was Todd going to be anything *but* ordinary, sitting on the bench? How was he ever going to break free and throw his hummer again unless he got in a game? Here was Benedict, screwing up the comeback of the best high school pitcher in the country, all for a little revenge.

By the time Bates got the third out I was so angry I didn't even know the score. Up at bat in the seventh I kept glancing at Benedict between pitches. He looked so damned pleased with himself it made me angrier still and I struck out, suckered by a curve a foot off the plate.

Just when I thought things couldn't get worse I spotted my dad in the stands. He must have come early from work; he had his briefcase beside him. I tried to look away, but he saw me and waved. I smiled weakly in return, ducked away and willed myself invisible.

When Tommy Ricco flied out to end the game I turned to Todd. He was staring at the field, idly playing with the plastic goggles dangling from his neck. I wondered if I should tell him what I had guessed about Benedict, but all that came out was, "My dad's here. You want a ride home?"

"That's okay." His voice came from far away.

"Oh, come on," I insisted. "I—"

"I'll see you tomorrow," he said, and bolted from the bench—almost as if he'd planned it, just then, when my cleats were off and I couldn't chase after him.

"Hey, Paulie," Dad's cheery voice rang out behind me.

"Hi, Dad." I looked right and left, anywhere but at him.

He smiled. "You got to play today."

"I stunk," I said.

"Oh," Dad frowned, "I wouldn't say you *stunk*. . . ."

That only made me feel worse. I would rather have heard *No you didn't*. But a strikeout and an error—Dad said what you had to, I guess, when you felt sorry for your kid but didn't want to lie.

I glanced behind the stands. Todd was already out of sight, over the hill toward home. But before I sank back to the bench, I paused. At the far corner of the stands there was the principal, Dr. Maethner, having it out with Benedict. I was too far away to tell what they were saying, except that neither was too happy with the other. Maethner, who walked through the halls at school shaking the hand of just about every kid who passed him, now pointed his finger at Benedict's chest, his face angry, his lips moving rapidly.

I thought again how Benedict had kept Todd a prisoner on the bench, and tried to fill in the words.

Harley pitched the next game, at Marshland. He did another good job, went the whole seven innings and only gave up three runs. After Harley, Spiros got another start, and we won that one, too. We were 3–1, with four days off till our next game, so Benedict could use Harley and then Spiros again and not worry about another starter. I'm sure that suited him just fine. By the third week of April we were 6–2. The local paper ran an article on what a surprise we were, since nobody had expected us to go anywhere after Todd's accident. Then a rain out jammed up our schedule and we had to play three games in four days.

"He'll have to pitch you on Tuesday," I whispered to Todd on the bus ride to Roaring Brook.

Todd smiled grimly. "Don't be so sure," he cautioned.

"What do you mean?" I said, too loud. Half a dozen faces turned my way. "What's he going to do? Spiros today, then Harley, and then what? He can't go with Spiros again, his dad'll have the whole Philharmonic out there picketing."

"Why should he pitch me?" Todd asked. "You saw how I threw the other day, at that scrimmage."

"You threw fine."

"Guys were hitting me."

"Yeah, because you were—"

"I know, I know, I was aiming the ball. I have to, Paulie. I'm wild, otherwise."

I jumped on that, exasperated. "You ought to just buzz the ball past them."

Todd said, "I just keep thinking of—"

166

"Of Rishi?" Todd nodded. "Look." I glanced over my shoulder and made Todd do the same, till we spied Rishi at the back of the bus. "Two days after you beaned him he got ninety-five on a math test. Maybe you ought to try that on me." Todd laughed, just a little. "Benedict has to pitch you," I said. "He's got no choice."

"He could start Bates."

"Bates?" I winced. "*Bates?*"

And that's just what he did.

With Bates on the mound, I got to play second again. I was glad, this time, not just to play, but because with Bates serving up his batting practice fastball it seemed we were in the field forever. Then I didn't have to sit by Todd and try to avoid his eyes.

By the sixth inning Foxwood had scored fifteen. If this was the perfect time to warm up Todd and let him pitch a little, Benedict acted as if the notion never occurred to him. He hardly moved, not even when Foxwood's leadoff batter slammed Bates's first pitch so far Tommy Ricco had to gallop all the way to the other diamond to track it down. The Foxwood fans were whooping it up so loudly by then I didn't think anybody but me noticed how Dr. Maethner picked his way down from the third row of the stands, leaned over the fence, and called out to Benedict.

Benedict didn't even turn his way. As the next batter dug in, I stole another glance at Maethner. His face now was dark red, and there was no denying: Benedict was doing his best to ignore him.

Maethner called to him a few more times, and then stepped

through the gate, scooted the freshman manager away, and took his spot on the bench—right next to Benedict.

On the field, a minor miracle: Bates threw a strike. A hoot or two came from the Foxwood side, but I could hardly pay attention to the game. Maethner was going at Benedict in that quiet, intense way that married couples fight when they're out in public, his voice full of whispers that should have been shouts. Still Benedict ignored him. His jaw clamped shut, he only jotted some detail in the score book.

I swung my head back just in time for the next pitch. When the Foxwood batter popped up to third, I looked again, but by then Maethner was gone.

The next day Benedict was late to practice and Coach Z set up some drills on his own. First he had me scuttling sideways like a crab, fielding imaginary grounders. After that I pitched batting practice. Without Benedict around I had a few laughs throwing my knurve until Tommy Ricco threatened me with a Louisville Slugger enema if he saw that pitch one more time. I didn't even notice the big blue Oldsmobile in the parking lot till it screeched to a sudden stop. Dr. Maethner, in his pin-striped blue suit, trotted toward us across the field. He headed straight for Coach Z, threw his arm around his shoulder, and drew him close for a conference.

Soon the whole team was watching how animated Maethner's face was, how he clapped Coach Z on both shoulders. Then Maethner called us over and announced that, as of today, Coach Zimler was taking over as the new varsity baseball coach.

"Of course Coach Benedict would have loved to continue

working with you all, but for . . ." Maethner hesitated a moment, "for *personal* reasons, he's decided to resign."

Maethner went on to say how nice it would be if we all took up a collection and got Coach Benedict a little something to show our appreciation. After all, he did take the team to the Eastern Regional Finals last season, and he was sure that each one of us had his own special memory of the coach. . . .

I didn't hear the rest, my heart was pounding so loud. All I could do was spot Todd, his face pale and unsure. I stared at him till he saw me. When he did, I felt a huge grin flare across my face, so bright I was afraid Maethner would see it and think I was mocking him. Finally, tentatively, Todd smiled in return.

The smile of a guy whose time had come.

Austin Wolfe was talking about a gift for Benedict, everybody kicking in. A little light-headed, as if I'd stood up too fast, I told him he could put me down for five.

"Now *there's* a story," Melissa beamed. We stood at her locker, the only one in the school with pictures of reporters taped inside the door. "We'll do a big personality piece on Coach Z." She frowned at me. "Maybe that will make up for how much hell I caught when Todd didn't start that first game like you said he would."

"Well, now he'll get his chance," I bubbled. "Coach Z *loves* Todd. He believes in him, like us. And once he starts him," my giddy tone soared above the other voices in the hall, "and people start noticing, and those scouts start coming back," I clutched her arms and shook her playfully, "you'll have more news than you'll know what to do with."

I stepped back, self-conscious about grabbing her like that. I could feel myself blushing, and said quickly, "I've got another article for you."

"Wait a minute. Paulie Lockwood is *volunteering* an article?"

"On Benedict. How he didn't resign for *personal reasons* at all."

Melissa looked bewildered. "He didn't?"

"He got *fired*," I said. "Maethner fired him. Because he wouldn't pitch Todd."

"Paulie," she said, her editor's instinct taking over. "How do you *know* that?"

I told her how I'd seen Maethner and Benedict, face-to-face, not once but twice.

"That doesn't mean anything," she said, but her voice rose at the end like a question.

"No?" I jumped in. "And both times, Todd just sitting on the bench while Bates was getting clobbered, and Edgeview getting *embarrassed*. . . ." I could see her start to think it over, and hurried on. "You know how he hates the school to look bad. . . ."

"That's right." She nodded. "How many times has he cut one of our articles because the *parents* might not like it?"

"See? And here Todd could be pitching, and Edgeview could be part of the biggest comeback in sports *history*—"

"But why *wasn't* he pitching?" she asked.

I shook my head. "Benedict was *jealous*, Melissa. He's always been jealous of Todd."

"But wouldn't it be a better team with Todd pitching?"

"Of course it would. I guess that didn't matter. He always knew Todd didn't need him. That riled him. And here was a way to get back."

She didn't even look angry, just sad. "I can hardly believe it."

"So here's the story," I said eagerly. "Maethner figured it out, stepped in and did the right thing. He fired Benedict." I waited a second or so, and said, "So can I write that article, too?"

She took forever to say, "You can't, Paulie."

"I can't? Why *not?*"

"You know why not—Maethner won't let us print it. Even if it is true. What kind of headline do you want? *Jealous Baseball Coach Sabotages Superstar?* Think he'll go for that?"

"I don't know. I thought, maybe . . ."

"Write the one on Coach Z. Make it good. Forget about Benedict."

I frowned. "I still think we're letting him off the hook."

"Maybe we are. But we can't solve everything. And meanwhile—"

"I know, I know." I said it with her. "We've got a newspaper to get out."

Chapter 17

My dad pulled me from Monday's practice, telling me how much I'd like this special, after-school intensive SAT prep class he had signed me up for. I tried to fight him, but he kept saying, "It's just three hours, Paulie. Three hours for your future." When I got out of the class that evening I was so dazed by multiple choice lists of six-syllable words that I didn't even hear the phone ring.

"Guess who's pitching Friday?" Todd asked, almost before I said hello.

I hooted in triumph, "I *told* you Coach Z knows talent." Then I started giggling, just at the thought of Todd out there on the mound. "Calm down, it's no big deal," he kept saying, but soon I had him giggling, too. For a while, before we hung up, we sounded like twin coyotes howling at the moon.

Now as our guys took the field for the Wednesday game against Westfield, I still felt as if I were in some kind of helium balloon; if I weren't tied down I'd be up above the treetops in no time. Todd taking the mound in two days. The team 12–5 now, with an excellent shot at the play-offs. With Coach Z in charge we had won our first two games. When he was just an assistant, Coach Z had always talked about all the offbeat moves they did in the old days, delayed steals and the hidden ball trick. Since Maethner named him boss there was none of that; we just won.

A lot of kids from Edgeview had come for the game, and the stands were packed. As Harley Shawn strutted around on the mound, I whispered to Todd, "Thank God for Coach Z, that's all I've got to say."

"Listen. . . ."

"Thank God *somebody's* a big enough guy he doesn't have to be *jealous*—"

"Last night"—Todd's tone dropped an octave—"an agent called."

My mouth suddenly gummed up on me. "An agent?"

"You remember Mr. Wylie, that guy I told you about, last spring?"

I shook my head.

"Rolex, zillion-dollar suit, limo so long you could stick a Cadillac in the trunk. . . ."

"What'd he say?" I choked.

"Said he just called to see how I was doing." Todd savored it as he told me. "Said he'd been waiting to see me pitch all spring."

"Did you tell him to thank Coach Benedict for that?"

Todd ignored my dig. "He said he was looking forward to getting together." He faced me, working hard to keep his smile in.

I could feel my eyes bulging out. "So did you tell him?" I croaked.

"Tell him what?"

"That you're pitching on Friday?"

"Paulie," Todd said calmly. "I'm surprised at you. Don't you think he knew?"

After that I could hardly pay attention to the game. We had the lead for a while, but then a couple of errors and a couple of walks let Westfield back in. Harley was storming around on the mound, glaring at his infielders, when the Engineers' big right-handed cleanup hitter, Wes Pollack, came to bat. Harley coiled, threw a chest-high fastball, and Pollack bashed it to the opposite diamond.

The guys on our bench all groaned—but not me. I leaned close to Todd. "Well," I cracked, nodding toward Harley, "the jayvee team always needs pitchers."

But he wasn't listening; he and everybody else were looking out at the field. I heard angry voices, and turned. Harley was standing at the foot of the mound, jawing at Pollack how he didn't like his home run trot. Pollack stepped on the plate, turned, and said something back. Harley must have cursed, for then Pollack was striding out toward the mound. Harley tossed down his glove and raised his fists, waiting. By then all the guys were on their feet. I stood up, too. Coach Z and Emo Tortelli were already out there, arms around Harley, the Westfield coach was holding Pollack back, and the ump was in the middle of it all, shouting and waving his hands.

174

Nobody had really run out onto the field—that was a great way in high school ball to get kicked off the team—but the guys on both sides were milling along the fence, talking tough. It wasn't a surprise to me. Harley's temper was always getting him in trouble. What surprised me was long after Coach Z ordered everyone back to the bench, Todd was still standing out there with some of the seniors, as if any moment now they were going to hop the fence and charge.

"What are you *doing?*" I grabbed his elbow and tugged him to the bench. "You want to get hurt? You want to get *thrown out,* so you don't pitch Friday?"

He shrugged me off, a little annoyed. "What, the whole team's standing there, I'm not supposed to?"

I dropped to the bench beside him, exasperated. "No," I chided him. "Not *now*. Not this close. The *team?*" I shook my head. "Just think about *Todd.*"

Near the end of practice on Thursday, while everyone else was running laps, Coach Z had me going over how to score from third on a fly ball. It was just what I didn't need. I was so nervous for Todd's start against Fox River I could hardly listen to him, but like a madman he kept drilling the steps into me: "The *ball* hits the glove, you *kick* off the bag, you *bore* your eyes in on home—"

I was even more distracted when I spied Melissa, leaning over the wire fence by the stands, watching us. The rest of the team was already changing out of their cleats, heading home.

"Okay if I take off, Coach?" I asked. He gave me one of

those *Kids today!* sighs, and waved me away. I hurried over to Melissa. When I recognized the printout of my Coach Z article in her hand, she couldn't keep back the grin.

"Paulie," she beamed. "This is great. You make Coach Z sound fascinating."

"Oh yeah?" It sure was fascinating tagging up at third, forty times in a row.

"You've got quotes, and anecdotes. You did some *work* for this one. I didn't know he played professionally."

"In the minors," I said. "For a season and a half."

"Well, see?" She smiled triumphantly. "Nobody would have known that." Her eyes softened. "And how he started coaching high school ball after his wife died, and how it helped him cope. That was beautiful."

"I didn't know," I shuffled my feet, "if you wanted that kind of stuff. . . ."

She waved the article. "We'll get a nice photo of the coach and"—she paused, folded her arms on the top of the fence, and rested her chin there. "Did you ever think about being a reporter?"

"Aw, come on." I turned aside, sure she was kidding me.

"I mean it."

I knew how amateurish my article on the practice field was, and how I practically made up the one on Todd starting the season opener. But this one I really had done some work on, staying late one day after practice, interviewing Coach Z, and writing it on Tyler's computer over several nights. It did have facts and quotes and all those things she nagged about. I said, "A reporter? You think so?"

"Sure I do." We drifted along the fence, on opposite sides, toward the parking lot. "Maybe you ought to start thinking about a good J-school."

"J-school?" I glanced over at her. "What's that?"

"That's what you call a journalism school," she said. "You know, at college."

We had reached the gate, but I didn't come through.

She must have seen something in my face. "Paulie, what's the matter?"

"I've got to go to *college* to be a *sports* reporter?"

"Of course you do." She laughed. "What'd you think, you"—she cut herself off. "You're serious, aren't you?"

"I'm not going to college." For a moment it made me feel like a little kid, trying out a curse word—some part of me was thrilled that I could say it.

"You'll get into college, don't worry," Melissa scolded, as if I were just being silly.

"I'm not talking about getting *into* college. I don't want to go, period."

We stood there, probably the only two people in the whole park by then. I fidgeted under her glance.

"So what *are* you going to do? If you don't go to college."

"Now you sound just like my dad." I rubbed my scalp angrily. "Maybe college isn't for everybody. Maybe some people should see that."

She looked me up and down. "This is about Todd, isn't it?"

Now I didn't like *her* tone. "That's got nothing—"

"You still think you'll just tag along beside him—"

"I don't think anything."

"—like you did when you were a freshman, and he was Todd, the big star." What irritated me most was the look of disappointment on her face. "You're not a freshman anymore."

"Yeah, well, Todd's still a big star. Or he will be, this Friday."

"And what'll you be, this Friday?"

"I'll be his friend."

"You always say that," she shouted. "As if it's the answer to everything. But you know what it is? It's an excuse. An excuse for not thinking for yourself."

I turned away from her. "I have to go," I said curtly. "I'm glad you liked the article."

Melissa grabbed my arm. "Paulie. What are you afraid of?"

"What the hell is *that* supposed to mean?"

"What if Todd doesn't make the pros? What if *he* goes to college?"

"Melissa, once they get a load of him on Friday, he won't have to go to college."

Her eyes never left me. "That's not what I asked."

"From the time he had the accident, there's only one thing Todd's been thinking about—baseball. Not *college.* He doesn't need to hear about *college.*" I could feel myself shaking. "All he needs is people to believe in him." I tried to stare her down. "I guess there aren't as many of those as I thought."

"That's not fair."

"Why do you want to give up on him now?"

"I'm not giving up. I wasn't even *talking* about Todd."

"So maybe he *won't* be the number one draft pick. Maybe he won't sign for a million bucks."

"I was talking about you," she said.

"Maybe some team'll take him in the eighth or ninth round and he'll work his way up from nowhere. And that'll be an even better story, won't it?"

She crossed her arms, exasperated with me.

"Maybe," I said, "somebody from J-school can write it."

Chapter 18

Todd was wrong: You could stick two Cadillacs into Mr. Wylie's limo. Before the game he leaned against the side of it, doing most of the talking while Todd stood there kneading his glove nervously.

I watched from the edge of the parking lot. Finally Wylie laughed, shook Todd's hand and picked his way to where his chauffeur had been saving him a seat in the stands.

But just as I started toward Todd, an old guy with a clipboard and a stopwatch around his neck got to him first. And then another guy in a suit showed up, and after that the Albany Eyewitness News van screeched to a stop. A videocam crew leaped out like terrorists on a mission, and the next thing I knew Todd was surrounded, with three other guys waiting for them to be through.

Finally I saw Coach Z, signaling for Todd to come warm up. Todd smiled at the reporters—for an instant I saw the polished skills he had learned from becoming a celebrity so young—and broke away politely. The videocam crew hustled to the field to set up for some game shots, and one or two reporters even tried to corner Coach Z.

Emo Tortelli was already warming Todd up when I took my

seat on the bench. I looked around. The stands were packed more than they ever were for a regular league game. I spied more reporters—or maybe they were scouts—up in the stands. In the top row I saw Mr. Wylie, and down the way a couple of guys in suits almost as flashy. And there were Todd's parents, and mine, Melissa (I was feeling so good I waved to show her no hard feelings from the day before) with some kids from the paper, Dr. Maethner and just about the whole faculty, even Benedict (so it was true, criminals *did* return to the scene of their crimes)—and people from town, everybody from the mayor and Mr. Guion, who owned the brake parts plant, down to the two dorky Laduzinsky brothers, who hadn't missed a game since *they* were in high school, however long ago that was. There were so many kids and parents that a sprawling collection of folding chairs and blankets had multiplied down both foul lines.

Then Todd was standing next to me, his jacket slung over his right arm. "You're all pale," he said to me. "You gonna be okay?"

"Me? Stop—" We both laughed as my voice croaked. "Stop worrying." Behind me Coach Z. was reading off the lineup. When he got to Todd's name, we grinned at each other. He stood up, shrugged off his jacket, and whacked me in the shoulder with his glove. "This one's for you, pal," he said.

When the Panthers took the field there was an explosion of sound. Even Harley had his cap tilted back as if he wanted to be sure to see. The Fox River players looked jittery. They'd probably never played before such a crowd.

There was Todd, taking his warm-ups, the force of his

follow-through carrying him a little toward first. Kicking the rubber between throws as he always had, deliberate. The ump yelled, "Play ball." Todd pulled off his glove, wiped his goggles, and took a couple of seconds to concentrate.

And while he did I traced back the invisible line from all these agents and scouts up in the stands, and the Six O'Clock News team, back through the Albany papers, the *Edgeview Gazette,* then *Panther Paws,* Melissa—to me. To Todd and me, out here on those frigid nights, when this was all a dream.

I opened my eyes and saw it just as it used to be: Todd on the mound, Melissa somewhere in the stands, me on the bench, and the sun shining bright.

Then Todd threw his first pitch.

Coach Z left him in till the fifth. Maybe he was waiting to see if one of those innings Todd was going to get mad and finally throw that good cheese, the fastball we all knew he had. He never did. Just that same old nothing pitch he'd been throwing since Rishi Patel got beaned. Soon enough the Fox River batters were pumping up for it, pulling sizzling line drives to left—one nearly decapitated Frankie Flynn at third. It was 10–4 by the fourth. Out of desperation Todd went to his curve, and when he didn't walk or hit somebody, you could see the Fox River guys timing its arrival and almost smiling as they swung.

It wasn't just falling way behind that sent Coach Z finally trotting out in the fifth, signaling Bates in from second to take over on the mound. It wasn't the two home runs that Ozzie Fuentes chased down, gasping as if he'd run a marathon.

No, Coach Z pulled him for a two-hop grounder back up the middle.

I saw it, too. How Todd brought his hands up to cover the side of his face and ducked away from an easy bouncer he could have fielded a year ago with—

Well, with his eyes closed.

When Coach Z made the pitching change he got some light boos, but soon there was a roar, loud and strong for Todd as he trudged down off the mound.

And then I heard my name.

Of course—Coach Z wanted me to fill in for Bates at second. He was calling me now to get out there. I grabbed my glove and raced onto the field. When Todd and I passed each other I knew I should look over, make some kind of reassuring sign. But I couldn't.

He didn't look my way, either.

There wasn't much time to worry about it; Fox River pounced on Bates immediately. When I finally got a chance to turn around and scan the stands, I noticed half the kids were gone, and Maethner, too, Benedict, most of the scouts, and for sure, Mr. Wylie.

Todd, too. Even Todd was gone.

After the game my dad got down to me pretty fast. I hadn't even taken off my cleats. We nodded, but neither of us spoke. If I were in third grade he would have just reached out and drew me to him in a big hug. You could tell he still wanted to; maybe I wanted him to as well.

"Pretty tough about Todd," he only said.

I dug furiously at a knot in my laces. "It's just one game."

He waited a little. "I know."

"It doesn't mean anything."

Even longer this time. "I know."

I got fed up and yanked the shoe off, threw it in my duffel bag, and handed the whole thing to Dad. "I need to go see him," I said. I jammed my feet into my sneakers. "I don't want a ride."

But he knew that, too, and didn't say a word to stop me.

All the way across the park and the four blocks after that, still in my uniform, I jogged to Todd's house. Mrs. Bannister sent me right up. I knocked at his door but didn't wait for an answer, and almost tripped over a mound of clothes as I went in. He was leaning against the headboard of his bed, shirtless, in an old pair of jeans.

"When you go"—he pointed a finger at the pile by my feet, and I looked again and recognized his balled-up uniform— "why don't you take that." His mouth trembled slightly. "I won't be needing it."

I pulled a chair to the side of the bed. "What's that supposed to mean?"

"What do you think?" He shook his head, and snorted something close to a laugh. "I'm not going through that again."

"Come on," I said. "You had a bad day—"

He looked incredulous. "A bad *day?*"

"Okay," I stammered. "All right. So—"

Then Todd was eerily calm, recollecting. "You know, I . . . I can't remember that ever happening before. Getting

184

taken out of a game." He leaned forward, suddenly intense as a predator. "Can you, Paulie? Can you remember me ever getting hit that hard?"

"No," I said hoarsely. "No, I can't."

"And you remember everything, don't you?" He lashed out, "You remember every game I've ever pitched. You know more about me than anybody."

I nodded.

Todd's good eye bored in on me. "So how come you never told me I stink?"

"You don't," I said softly.

"I *stink*. I had *nothing* out there today." He leaped off the bed, strode to the wall, slammed both hands against it and turned on me. "You still won't admit it."

"Because it's not true. You can't tell from one game. . . ."

"Think Mr. Wylie couldn't tell?"

"Stop it," I murmured.

"So take that in for me tomorrow, will you?" He pointed to the clumped-up uniform by the door. "Then I won't have to see Coach Z, or anybody else."

I had a vision of carrying in his uniform like someone's remains, and shook my head. "I'm not your servant."

His lips formed something too cruel to be a smile. "Weren't we going to call it *personal assistant*?"

I ignored that. "You're not throwing the way you can."

"It's too late for that."

"You're not. It's like you really don't *want* to try." My voice gathered an angry momentum. "You just want to play it *safe*, that's all."

"Safe?" His eyes narrowed.

"You know." I gave in a little. "Instead of throwing your—"

"I'm playing it safe."

"Look. Forget I said that. What we have to do now—"

"What *we* have to do?" Todd put his face right in mine. "*We* don't have to do anything, Paulie. *I* do. It's Todd Bannister out there. Stop talking like you're part of this."

"There's still a chance," I said, my voice raspy. "It's not like Benedict's still here. He's gone. And Coach Z knows you can pitch, and—"

"You're right." Todd smiled darkly. "Benedict's gone. No wonder you were so happy about that. You're the one who's safe."

"What's that supposed to mean?"

"Don't you remember the list on the bulletin board last fall, the cut list?"

"Yeah," I muttered. "So?"

"So what'd you think, the next day, when suddenly you were on the other list? Did you think all of a sudden Benedict realized what a *clutch hitter* you were? Don't you know what happened?"

I could feel cold sweat start to trickle under my arms.

"I got Benedict to keep you on the team."

"You got—" I looked up. "But how?"

"It was easy," he smirked. "I told him I wouldn't play without you."

"That's . . ." my voice faltered, and my stomach dropped away. "You're making that up." But I knew he wasn't. I thought of that health class two years ago when Todd had threatened to quit, and Benedict had buckled under, even then. "You did that for me?"

He didn't look particularly pleased about it. "Yeah."

My legs felt as light as papier-mâché just then, too weak to push me up and out of the chair.

"So stop saying I'd be the same as ever if it weren't for Benedict. Stop making him the bad guy. There isn't a bad guy in this, okay? There's just this." In one quick move he lifted his right lid with one hand and seemed to rip out the prosthesis, cupping it casually in his open palm so I was sure to get a good look.

I'd seen him take it out lots of times, but never like that. As if the whole point were to gross me out.

I stood up, and tried to steady myself.

"I'll tell Coach Z," I said. "And I'll come by . . . and get this." I gestured to his uniform. "I'll get it later."

He frowned. "You don't have to."

"No," I said. "I want to." I took a deep breath. "You're right. It was just you out there today. I guess I never thought of it that way."

"Paulie, wait." Todd laid the prosthesis on a paper towel. "I'm sorry. I shouldn't have told you that, about getting you on the team. That was out of line."

My eyes locked on his. "But it's true, isn't it? I wouldn't be on the team without you."

"Yeah." He backed off a step. "It's true."

I nodded, and felt my shoulders sag.

"All right," he said abruptly, too eager, too loud. "I'll stay. All right? I'll stay on the team."

I waved it away. "Do what you want."

"No, I'll stay." His chin tightened. "I'll—I'll keep trying."

"Whatever," I shrugged.

"Well, it's *hard,* damn it," he shouted. "Don't you see how hard it is?"

I stood at his door. "How about that guy you told me about?"

"What guy?"

"That Herb Score. Don't you think it was hard for him?"

"Oh yeah. Herb Score." Todd sat at his desk and squirted some cleaner on his prosthesis. "Well, there's one thing about old Herb I didn't mention, Paulie." He turned quickly, his face bitter again. "He stunk. Ever since the accident. He made it back, but he stunk. For five crummy years."

"At least," I could hardly manage a whisper, "he didn't give up. He was . . . He was courageous."

"That's great," Todd said. "He was courageous, and he stunk. That's a lot to look forward to."

Part Four

JUST LIKE THE
LADUZINSKY BROTHERS

Chapter 19

The team is really rolling now. . . .

The team is on a roll. . . .

The team is on a march to . . .

The Panthers are marching to the county play-offs for sure. . . .

I shut my eyes and leaned forward until my head thunked
on the monitor. Starting the article wasn't a problem; starting
was easy. But somewhere, lurking, was the sentence I didn't
know how to write. It went something like *Much of the Panthers' success is due to the ace pitching of senior standout Harley
Shawn, junior Spiros Demopolous, . . .*

The hard part was the finish.

. . . and senior Todd Bannister.

Oh, I could write it, I guess. It just wouldn't be true.

"You know what we need?" Melissa had ambushed me in
the cafeteria line the day before. "We need an article on how
good the team is doing."

I stared at the ravioli special. "Everybody knows how good
they're doing."

"That's right," Melissa countered with a laugh. "So they'll
be sure to read it. Do I have to explain *everything?*" Then she
was already down the line with her tray, passing people like an

impatient driver. She called back, "I need it Thursday, okay?" and didn't wait for an answer.

And here I was, wondering how I could write something that didn't sound sour or whiny or as if I were on leave from the obituary department. That's how excited I was about the team.

Coach Z had given Todd another start a week after the Fox River game, against Lansford, but it didn't go any better. Whatever good stuff he still had from before the accident he wasn't showing. His fastball sailed in on a flat line, as if he were afraid to let it rip. And the curve was worse. It either sent the batter sprawling or Emo Tortelli leaping wildly to knock it down.

How had we fooled ourselves, I wondered, those February evenings working out on our own? Thinking Todd could lose an eye and still fling the ball right on target at ninety miles an hour. It was pitiful, really, just like all my faith in Coach Z. *He believes in you, Todd. That's why he gave you a chance.* Yeah, right, that and orders from Maethner. He was nothing, I saw, like the colorful character Melissa had raved about in my article. He was just a nice old guy, so eager to run the varsity he'd do anything Maethner told him to—even play a kid he knew had no business being out there.

The next time Todd pitched was the seventh inning of a laugher where we had a 9–1 lead. They rocked him for three quick runs before Rishi hauled in a couple of long drives in right and everybody sighed in relief. And while some of the guys were strutting around and whooping it up about being *this close* to the play-offs, all I could think of was how Todd wouldn't have had to go through any of this, how he would have quit the team two weeks ago—if not for me.

I blinked, and tried to stare down the computer. I didn't have to write about the pitchers, I supposed. I could mention Tommy Ricco's six home runs, or Bates's .463 average. But I'd pull one way, and the sentences would tug the other, and all the while I heard myself muttering *So what? Big deal. Who cares?*

Finally I blipped off the whole screen in disgust, shoved back my chair, and stormed out of the computer center. At the door I nearly crashed into Melissa.

She wore a baggy Columbia sweatshirt with the sleeves rolled up, in her arms a book bag and overstuffed notebook. When she had that ready-to-work intensity she seemed to glow.

"Paulie, look at this." She tore open the book bag zipper, pulling out a tiny black taperecorder. "The Dictaphones came in."

"Uh-huh." I nodded, looking past her. "That's great."

"The paper got two," she said. "So you can use one," she held it out to me, "when you're doing an article. You can get your quotes this way and then you don't have to—"

"I don't need that," I said.

"Sure you do. I—" She lowered the Dictaphone. "What's wrong—that article on the team? So take a few more days on it." She smiled and offered the Dictaphone again. "Here."

My hands burrowed into my pockets. I shook my head. "I'm not doing the article." I crossed my arms, dipped my head, and finally looked back at her. "I . . . I just can't do it."

"It's *easy*," she scolded me. "You know how. You've written—"

"Stop telling me I can write." I felt something rise from my stomach, bitter as heartburn. "What is it, you feel sorry for me?"

Melissa stepped back, wary. "Paulie, what's the matter?"

"There aren't going to be any more articles, okay? God, Melissa, who cares how well the team's doing?"

She paused, as if she were committed to wring out every last bit of patience. "Don't you care the team's winning?"

The team? Should I tell her how little I had to do with the team? I wondered, was there one single thing I had ever done that somebody hadn't helped me on? *Todd* got me on the team. *Melissa* printed what I had pawned off on her as articles. If there were a way, *my dad* would probably take the SATs for me himself—or worse, send Tyler.

"The team," I only said, "just doesn't seem very important right now."

She ran a hand through her hair. "You're thinking about Todd, aren't you?"

But I wasn't, not the way she meant. I was thinking about me.

"You spent all that time, working with him, and now, his last two games—"

Not Todd, Melissa, *me*. Seven months broken up and she still saw him when she looked at me. Well, why wasn't I happy? Wasn't that what I had wanted?

"You must feel—"

"You were a part of this, too," I snapped at her. I would have said anything then, just to hurt her. "You made a few phone calls."

"I made one."

"You ran that headline about Todd pitching. You knew it was bogus."

"You told me—"

"But you knew. Didn't you? So you were a part of this."

"Okay," she sighed in frustration. "You're right. And you know what? I wish I hadn't done it. I think we hurt Todd more than we helped him."

"We didn't help him at all," I mumbled.

"Maybe you're right." She readjusted her book bag and notebook for about the fourth time. "But our lives go on, you know."

"You mean *yours* goes on. Well, good for you. Go to Columbia. Go to J-school."

"Excuse me," her words sizzled with restraint, "for thinking about the future. Excuse me for thinking a little about my—" She took a step away, then spun around for one last word. "So tell me what Paulie Lockwood's going to do with his life, while he's criticizing everybody else?"

I shifted my weight uneasily.

"You know, Todd's a senior, Paulie. Do you ever think of that?"

"I know he's a senior."

"So what are you going to do when he's gone?"

"Maybe," I groped for an answer, "maybe he won't be gone."

"Everybody leaves, Paulie. Nobody stays in high school forever."

"Maybe he'll stick around." And then I thought of them, in the corner of the stands where they sat at every home game. "Maybe we'll be just like the Laduzinsky brothers."

Melissa's face softened. "Who?"

Nobody knew exactly how old they were—their thirties? Their fifties? But with their crewcuts, their T-shirts snug over their pot bellies, suspenders holding up droopy jeans, they looked like gargantuan nine-year-olds. They worked at night or didn't work at all, and some said they were retarded, and some said they were drunks, but mostly everyone was just used to them. At every home game they were in the stands, four rows up and all the way to the right, drooling tobacco juice, elbowing each other over some private joke, catcalling the umps. And they looked happy. That was the thing. They looked happy.

"The Laduzinsky brothers," I repeated, and my voice perked up with a crazy confidence. "Nobody'll bother us then," I continued, "about what we're going to *be,* or where we're going to *go.* 'Cause we're already there, see?" I walked away from her, just like that. "We're already there."

It was late, and I should have been in bed. The next day I had a big chemistry test and a game in the afternoon.

Neither seemed to matter much.

Instead of going to bed I fiddled with my dad's old shortwave radio, aiming the aerial at different walls until the wash of voices settled into something I could understand: a game.

That Cleveland station again. The same announcer I'd tuned in before. He had a good, warm baseball voice. *"Here we go, ninth inning, Indians up by two. Let's see if they can hold this lead...."*

I hunkered down by the radio and made the best of what was left.

That was when my dad knocked lightly, and came in. The first thing he must have seen was my chem text on the desk. "Hitting the books, huh?" he asked. But then he saw me by the radio.

"Just checking out a game," I said with a shrug. He sat down next to me on the bed and actually listened for half a minute, as if a Cleveland-Seattle game in early May were anything important.

Then he cleared his throat, and I noticed the two huge books tucked casually under one arm. He reached across me and turned the volume down a notch, though Seattle had the tying run on second.

"Found a new one today that might come in handy," he said, and dropped one of the books on my lap. I glanced at the cover. *A Guide to the SATs*. Because Dad was watching, I thumbed through it. Eight thousand pages, with tiny print, just like all the others he'd bought me. He asked, "How's it going on those practice tests I got for you?"

"Going good," I mumbled.

"What do we have, just two more days till the exam?"

"Uh-huh."

"You know, Paulie, it occurred to me—you're doing so much work on the computer these days. . . ."

"I am?" From the radio the announcer's voice squawked excitedly; I strained to hear him.

"Sure you are." He pulled out the other book—it was even bigger—and balanced it on his thigh. *Computer Shopper*, I read. "With those newspaper articles—"

I rolled my eyes. "Yeah. Three whole articles."

"Well, still," Dad smiled encouragingly, "your mother and I are happy to see you do it, and we thought, since Tyler's always playing those games on his computer, how about if we move the downstairs unit up here, to your room?" He glanced over. "We could put it on your desk."

Puzzled, I felt my brow grow tight.

He glanced around at my desk, empty now but for the unopened chemistry book. "I mean," he teased, "there's a lot of room."

"I guess," I said. "I don't mind."

"That way you wouldn't have to bother Tyler, and . . . well," he thumbed to a page in the thick catalog, "we're thinking of getting this model here, and then we'd put that downstairs. . . ."

I glanced at the colorful page. What he really wanted, I could tell, was to buy that new system. I tried to act interested.

"You're sure now? I mean, this is your room. It's your decision."

I looked at the desk, where for years, ever since I was nine, I've played Tabletop. I thought of all the player cards, all the major leaguers I had held in my hands. How I used to manage the teams, and feel so great about having this guy bunt or that guy steal second. That was the best part about it, to make the decisions—to feel myself in charge.

But I wasn't, of course. Even in Tabletop, I still had to roll the dice. A guy might pitch a perfect game—or he might give up ten runs in five innings. There was no guarantee.

What was it Melissa had asked me that day after practice? *What are you afraid of?*

I raised my eyes to Dad, waiting beside me on the bed. He was tired, his chin all five o'clock shadow, his hair rumpled. In the light of my bedside lamp his white shirt was the color of dust.

Dad slapped the catalog shut. "Well, we can think about it. We've got time."

"Plenty of time," I agreed.

"By the way," Dad cleared his throat, "I won't be able to make it to Thursday's game. I have a meeting, and—"

"That's okay," I said.

"But you've got one Saturday, right? In the afternoon, after the SATs? So I'll be at that one. And if I'm lucky, I can make the rest of your schedule—"

"Dad, listen," I interrupted. "You don't have to come."

He smiled uncertainly. "Paulie, I want to come."

"I know," I said. "What I mean is—I wish . . . you wouldn't come."

He let my words hang there for a couple of seconds before he spoke. He didn't even sound mad. "Why?"

Just tell him, I thought. How you wouldn't even be on the team in the first place if it weren't for your best friend, and just about every time you put your glove on now you knew you didn't just stink, you were a fraud as well.

"Why don't you want me to come?"

I heard the hurt tone in his voice, and I realized as hard as it was for me to say those things, it would be harder for him to hear them.

So I answered, "Because of Todd."

199

"Todd?"

"He—he might pitch that day. And he's had some bad luck—"

"I know."

"And . . . he doesn't want people to see him anymore, when he pitches. He's embarrassed, that's what he is."

"Well, what about the game after that?"

I shook my head. "No, see, we don't know when Coach Z is going to use him for relief. An inning here, or there. . . ." Finally I raised my glance to meet his. "Okay?"

Dad hunched over in thought. "Well." He rose slowly from the bed. "I don't want to make Todd uncomfortable." He stretched out his hand to rough up my hair, and for a second left it lying there. "You get some sleep, huh?" he said, and closed my door quietly.

For a long time I stared at the door after he had left. At some point I took notice of the game on the radio, faint but still audible. Seattle had tied it up, and they were going into extra innings. I switched off the light, lay back, and stared at the ceiling. Once or twice I might have dozed off, but by the top of the thirteenth I was still listening. *"This game might go forever,"* I heard the announcer say. *"That's the great thing about baseball, there's no clock. It's as if we could make time stand still."*

Okay with me, I thought.

Chapter 20

On the morning of the SATs I made it all the way to the school, to the foot of the steps that led up to the main entrance, and there, like a beat-up car conking out on the highway, I coasted to a stop.

I only had to lift my foot six inches to get on that first step, and the other foot would follow, and I could probably make it all the way in.

But I wasn't going to.

From behind me I heard a snort of annoyance as a kid almost bumped into my back. He stepped around me, muttering.

I wasn't afraid, exactly. There was just some kind of voice telling me not to go in, and I listened to it. I don't know how long I must have stood there, but it was long enough to stop counting the kids that passed me by.

Then I heard a voice, a real voice call a name, and I turned.

The funny thing was, the name wasn't mine.

I saw Chuckie Miles and another guy, and Chuckie said, "*Come on,* Lockwood. Frank *Thomas,* 1994."

I shook my head, blinked hard.

"Look at that." Chuckie laughed, and turned to his friend. "I knew I'd stump him sometime. I *knew* I would." He patted me on the shoulder and began to move past. "Hey, don't be so nervous, Lockwood. It's only the SATs."

But I wasn't nervous, I thought, as I watched Chuckie disappear into the building. I just didn't know the answer.

For the first time in my life, I didn't know.

I started to back up then, and all the time I never once took my eyes from the school. Across the street there was a bench near the bus stop. I collapsed into it and watched the last few kids rush inside. Soon there wasn't a sound from the school. It was even peaceful.

Six buses later (only one of the drivers really noticed me. "You getting on?" he asked) I knew the exam must have been over. The kids came out in clusters, and their voices filled the neighborhood. A few stood around, searching for friends. I could hear them asking about certain questions, and lots of groans and giddy laughter. But they didn't stay long. Some went to the parking lot, and some shuffled down the street, and some even came and stood by me, waiting for a bus.

That was what got me. How everybody seemed to know exactly where to go.

Who would have guessed that the guy who twice scored the winning run in the last week of the schedule, the runs that got us into the sectionals for sure, was me? That in the first game I would single and sneak to second on a poky outfielder's throw, then slide one way while the shortstop waved his glove the other? Or the following day against Addison, I'd race home on a sacrifice fly?

And who would have guessed that with the whole team shouting my name afterward and mobbing me at the plate, I didn't care one bit.

I didn't care. Before Coach Z sent me in I had just slouched next to Todd and hardly watched the game. From time to time I'd lean back to catch a glimpse of the Laduzinsky brothers in the stands behind us. Same spot as ever, four rows up and all the way to the right. They were chortling as usual, making up nicknames for the players on the other team. "Get a load of those guys." I nudged Todd, grinning. "You ever see two bigger goofs?" He took a quick peek, nodded, and turned back to the field.

It should have been a thrill when I got to play in the late innings. It wasn't. Not even in the Addison game, the score tied in the seventh, when I was out at second in place of Bates. I scooped up a hot shot to my right and nipped the batter at first, but as soon as I glimpsed Todd on the bench, his goggles hanging from his neck, I heard that voice again. The same one I heard the morning of the SATs. It was more a long, whispered sigh this time. *Who cares?* the voice kept saying. *Who cares?*

I heard it all the while I batted, even when I drew a walk and took my lead at first. When Chip Tunis slapped a pinch-hit single I made it all the way to third. Then Emo Tortelli lifted a high fly to left. "Tag up, tag up," I heard Coach Z yell. I watched my foot wedge itself sideways against the bag, as if it didn't need me to tell it what to do. When the leftfielder's glove gobbled up the ball my body took it from there, twisting and shoving off. My legs churned beneath me, my throat burned for breath, and when I slid home the dirt exploded around the plate. I hopped to my feet, and knew I was safe.

The whole team swarmed around me. There were shouts and hugs and high fives. I did my best to look enthused, but it was hard.

Somewhere on that run for home I had recognized the voice.

Now that we had clinched a spot the whole school was going nutty over the sectionals. On Saturday we were slated to play Westfield Tech at the community college field over at Hazelton. There was a pep rally Wednesday afternoon, and each morning during homeroom Dr. Maethner got on the intercom and shouted, "Let's go, Panthers" so loud the words disintegrated into blaring feedback. Every time you looked there were kids snipping out corny cardboard gloves and bats and balls and hanging them from the light fixtures in senior hall.

We still had one game left, on Friday against Dakinsville. Coach Z even let Todd pitch the last two innings. Spiros had a big Youth Symphony or something the next day and had to leave to rehearse after the fifth. Todd wasn't so bad; he only gave up a couple of runs. "Way to go, Todd," I called from second when Coach Z put me in for Bates. But all the time I kept thinking, So what? So he gets an out in the seventh inning of a doesn't-mean-anything game. And with every pitch he threw, the so-what's just kept adding up.

After dinner that Friday I was up in my room, waiting for Todd to stop by as he'd said he would. I needed somebody just as sick of the whole week of school spirit as I was, somebody I could drop my rah-rah face around and say, You know, the team's not that good, really. And who the hell cares if they are?

I heard my mom holler out, "Company, Paulie," and then quick footsteps up the stairs. "About time," I muttered, leaping off the bed to throw open the door.

When I found Melissa standing there I yelped like a Chihuahua.

She marched past me, into the room. Already I could tell she was boiling.

"You know," she began, a little stiffly, as if she had a whole rehearsed speech, "I am so fed up with you."

I was ready for a quick surrender. "Fed up about what?"

"Last week, you were such a jerk in the library."

"I know. Hey, I'm sorry."

But no little *sorry* was stopping her now. "And I let you get away with it. Because I wanted that article."

"Article?" I sank to the edge of my bed.

"The article on the team," she snapped. She paced all the way to the window and spun around quickly. "But since the *sectionals* start tomorrow, and I still haven't gotten a *single article* on the team from my *baseball writer* . . ."

I ducked my head.

"I guess I don't *have* to hold back anymore. I can tell you exactly what I think about you, Paulie, now that I don't have anything to lose." She placed her hands on her hips, stared coolly down at me. "You are—"

And then she stopped. She turned to her right and then her left, looked behind her, then over my shoulder.

"What is it?" I asked.

"Your room," she said. "The walls are so bare." I followed her gaze, a little surprised myself—as if it were somebody else and not me who had pulled down the pennants, junked the old posters and magazines pages, pried the tacks out till his thumb-nails ached. I heard her say, "It's just like Todd's."

"Aw," I waved, "it's not—wait a minute." I rose to my feet, facing her. "Since when were you in Todd's room?"

"I wasn't," she threw back at me. "You told me about it, re-member? How he took down all his awards? The trophies and the photographs?"

"Oh." I slumped back on the bed. "Right."

"What's that supposed to mean?" she attacked. " 'Since when were you in *Todd's* room?' "

Just then I heard Tyler clumping up the stairs. I rested my forehead in one hand and sighed. Just what I needed. He'd poke his head in, see me with Melissa, back out, and not say anything till she left. Then I'd hear kissy-smooch sounds every time he passed my door for the next week.

"Well?" Melissa pressed.

The footsteps paused just as I knew they would, by the door. I cringed. And then I heard a knock.

Tyler never knocked.

"*What?*" I snarled.

Peering around the door, about a foot above where Tyler's head should have been, Todd's eyes grew wide when he saw Melissa.

"Oh," he mumbled. "Hi."

"Where've *you* been?" I all but yelled.

He looked at me. "Hey, Paulie." Right away his eyes went back to her.

"How are you, Todd?" Melissa was backed up at my desk, groping behind her for my chair. When she found it she plunked herself down and pinned her hands between her thighs.

"I'm okay," he said, working on a smile. "I'm good." I could tell he was nervous; his fingers drummed at his sides. "Wow." He twirled in a complete circle, staring at my walls. "Paulie. What'd you do to—"

"Could everybody," I growled, "just *shut up* about my room?"

That got Todd and Melissa snickering, and for a minute they acted like toy robots who had just had their batteries replaced, twitching and fidgeting, and giggling at me. Todd's eyes flitted toward Melissa for just an instant, then darted away. "So, uh, how are you?" he finally asked her.

My voice grew sharp. "Melissa was just telling me how happy she is the team's doing so well."

There it was, a big opening for Todd to be as sarcastic as I was, and he missed it completely.

"They are doing well," Melissa offered.

He nodded. "Definitely."

"Thanks to Todd and me," I said.

He didn't even look my way. He glanced over at her shyly, and the next thing I knew they were talking Senior Talk. *Only a month left, huh?* and *I can't wait till graduation.* How far could they go with that, I thought, and made a big show out of examining my nails while I waited them out.

Then Melissa took a breath, hesitated, and asked him about his eye.

"It looks good," she added quickly. "It looks great." Todd blushed and said thanks, and she said something about what a tough year he'd had. He shrugged, "Aw, I guess." I almost had to laugh, how they were falling all over themselves to see who could be most polite.

Finally I looked up. "So," I said, my voice way harsh and loud—but it didn't matter. They wouldn't have heard anything just then. They were stuck in one of those *looks*—sizzling and secret, as if it could burn down walls, it was that intense.

My jaw dropped low. I'd seen that look a million times before they broke up, that dopey, glazed expression, as if they were communicating in some private language that left the rest of us out.

So I'd been right all along. All I should have done was just get them in the same room somehow. And now, that it was really happening—

I was jealous. That's what it was. Any moment they'd be kissing—why not, they'd always kissed right in front of me, I was just Paulie, after all—and my heart pounded in panic. I couldn't bear it if they did. Because I *didn't* want him back with her. And at the thought I felt slimy and small.

But they didn't kiss. They finally blinked and looked away. It wasn't because they got self-conscious that I was there. I was never there, I knew, no matter how much they let me tag along.

Todd mustered a grin. "I heard you're going to Columbia. That's a great school. Congratulations. That's great."

"Thanks," Melissa said softly, and looked up timidly to ask, "How about you? Have you—are you . . ."

"I'm going upstate," Todd told her. "I'm going to SUNY Plattsburgh."

It didn't even hit me at first, the way he went right on. "They have a pretty decent business school. My dad knows some people who went there. We thought I might like it."

I said, "You're going *where?*"

"Plattsburgh." He half turned my way. "I guess I never told you."

"No." I stared at him. "You never did."

"That's wonderful," Melissa said. Todd smiled, grateful for anything that let him ease away from me. "I know somebody who goes there," she said, and they joked a little about how cold he'd be in winter. Finally Melissa's voice trailed off. For the first time in five minutes, she noticed me. I must have been quite a sight, glaring at Todd. "Well, I've got to go," she said, and sprang to her feet. "I'll see you, Paulie." I wasn't going to look at her—but at the last second I gave in. By then she had paused in front of Todd. "I guess . . . you know, we'll talk again. . . ."

"Sure." He nodded quickly. "Sure we will."

She leaned in, awkwardly pecked him a quick kiss on the cheek, gave him half a hug, and whispered something.

We waited till her footsteps led down to the front door. Todd paced casually to the far wall. I let almost a minute go by, and finally the silence drove him to say, "Don't start, okay?"

"I can't believe you never told me."

"I was going to tell you," he shrugged. "What'd you think, I—"

"You must have known for weeks. Maybe *months*. And you still didn't tell me, it just slipped out."

"Listen." He checked his watch. "Maybe I'll just head on home. Coach wants us there at noon tomorrow, right?"

I rose, crossed my arms, and angled myself just enough to block his way to the door. "What are you going to do at college," I asked, "studying *business?*"

"I don't know." He grabbed his jacket from the back of my chair. I didn't budge.

"Since when are you interested in *business?*"

"I don't know what I'm interested in." His back stiffened. "That's why I'm *going* to college, okay?" He tried to squeeze past. "I'll see you," he mumbled. I waited a second, then backed off, threw on a sweater and started down the stairs after him.

He looked up at me. "What are you doing?" he asked.

"It's Friday night," I sneered. "Don't *friends* always hang out on Friday night?"

He didn't answer. By then we were in the downstairs hall-way. In the living room my dad and mom and Tyler were all sitting silently on the couch, as if they had stopped talking the moment they heard us coming down. There was something about the scene that made me linger, but Todd had already waved to them and was through the front door. "I'm going out for a little while," I called, and they all nodded (even Tyler), and *that* was weird—as if they were waiting for me to go.

Todd was already a couple of houses down the block. I trotted to catch up. "So," I said, with a phony kind of cheer. "Where *are* we going?"

Todd hunched up his shoulders. "Knock it off."

"Hey, I've got an idea," I chirped. I was way past reining myself in; it felt good to be so snide. "It's still light out. Let's grab our gloves and head for the park." I scowled at him. "We can work on your *comeback.*"

Maybe Todd should have just decked me and ended it there. For a second nothing moved in his face. Then he sighed, shook his head, and brushed past.

"Come *on,*" I yelled at his back, and when he didn't stop I hurried after him. "See, that's what's wrong with you." I could feel the sarcasm hissing out of my voice the way a bike rider knows his tire's going flat. "You gave up."

He paused at a corner of the busy street, and then, without a moment's hesitation, loped across.

"You gave up," I said, trailing him to the edge of the park. "You didn't know how hard it would be."

"Leave me alone," I heard him mutter.

"You didn't believe," I continued, "and as soon as it got tough—"

"What are you *talking* about?" He pivoted so quickly we almost collided. "I didn't *believe?* I tried, and it didn't work out, okay?"

"Yeah," I sputtered, "you believed so much you were sneaking off applying to places like SUNY Plattsburgh, just in case—"

"Just in case I didn't make it. And I didn't, did I?"

"How *could* you make it, if all the time your mind was on something else?"

"You're just mad," Todd shouted, "because I'm doing something with my life, and there's nothing in it for you, is there?"

I stepped back. "What do you mean?"

"There's nothing *glamorous* about just having a friend in college. You can't be his *personal assistant* there."

"I ought to punch you for that."

"Did you ever think maybe *that's* why you cared so much? So you could be something, too?"

I made my mouth a hard line, and didn't answer.

"And that was okay," he went on haltingly. "It would have been fun to have you along, you know? But now . . . I'm going somewhere else. . . ."

"Yeah," I mocked hoarsely. "Plattsburgh."

"And you won't let me go there. You won't let me get past the trophies and the agents, and being Todd the big star." His voice grew shaky. "I've got to get past that now. And it's hard."

"What you need—"

"No," he shouted. "Don't say it."

"What you need," I raised my voice to top his, "is to *keep trying.* To throw your goddamn fastball *like it's all you've got in the whole world.*" We had come to the edge of the park. I saw myself, three months ago, shadowing Todd to his secret workouts. "Remember when you were coming here at night? Nothing was going to stop you then," my words quivered with anger, "because you *believed.* . . ."

"Oh, *stop it,*" Todd howled with pain. "Stop loading all that

212

on me, okay? I can't do it." His voice caught and he blinked away tears. "Even with your help, Paulie."

"Why didn't you *tell* me?" I demanded. "About Plattsburgh? About going to college?"

"I didn't think I could."

"What?"

"Listen to me." He squared himself to face me. "I don't need a friend who only reminds me how great I *used* to be. I need a friend who can see me the way I am."

I stared at the sidewalk. "How great you used to be," I said. "Just listen to yourself. That's why you didn't make it back. You stopped believing."

"Paulie," he sighed, exasperated.

"*Everybody* stopped believing. You and Melissa and Coach Z and all those stupid scouts and agents. Everybody—except for me."

"And it wasn't even your dream, was it?" He smiled sadly. "When are you going to get one of your own?"

"That's my business," I said curtly.

"Okay." He nodded. "But if you think you still believe, you're wrong." He turned to go, and held back. "You just *don't* believe in anything else."

I stood and watched him go, and when he was out of sight I roamed all through the park, past the playground and the swimming pool, and I ended up where I knew I would all along, at the diamond. There were a couple of kids playing catch along the third base line, though it was getting dark by then. I leaned against the backstop, watching them. After a while I climbed up into the stands on the first base side. I climbed four rows up and all the way to the right. Even in the dusk I could see the brown flecks of dried tobacco juice, spattered everywhere. I slid my butt around, crossed one leg, then the other, then propped my feet up on the seat below, leaned on an elbow, leaned forward, rested my arms on my knees and braced my chin. I must have squirmed around like that for five minutes, and never did get comfortable.

By the time I looked up, the kids were gone.

Chapter 21

When I got home my dad was the only one up, watching TV with all the lights off. My stomach was gnawing me away from the inside out, and I thought something to eat might quiet it down. All I had to do, though, was poke through the fridge for a second to know I wouldn't be stifling this feeling with food.

Then for a moment, while I lingered by the table, I realized how exhausted I was. I slumped to a chair as if I had to rest just to make it upstairs. Dad came through the hallway and took a seat across from me. "All excited about the game?" he asked.

"Yeah." Maybe I could have gotten away with that. My mistake was when I added, "I guess."

Dad's eyebrows rose. He cocked his head to one side. The humming of the kitchen light fixture was the only sound in the house.

"You guess?"

"Well . . . I mean. . . ." I twisted painfully. "I *want* to be. . . ." And then I just lost it. He heard a quaver in my voice and his whole face changed; all this *concern* swept in and the instant I saw that I felt as if I were a little kid again. "I want to be"—a big sob seemed to shake me in half and I had to wait for it to clear—"but I can't. . . ."

Dad leaned closer, as if to lay a hand on my arm, but held back at the last second. All it did was remind me how pitiful I was, sixteen years old and blubbering like this.

He asked, "Because of Todd?"

I scoffed, "Todd?" as if it were the most ridiculous suggestion in the world. And then I told him. How Todd was going off to Plattsburgh. "He kept the whole thing a secret," I said, "like he knew he was doing something sneaky." The way Todd looked as he walked away from me at the park, that closed-off stranger's stare, I told him that, too. By the time I was finished my body sagged in the kitchen chair like a pile of laundry.

"You're right," Dad said at last. "He should have told you."

I wrung my hands. "It's like I don't even know who Todd *is* anymore."

He nodded. "Maybe Todd doesn't know, either. Maybe he's trying to find out. That doesn't have to change anything between you two."

"Well, it has."

"So . . . maybe it's time to find out who Paulie Lockwood is."

I laughed sourly.

"What's the matter?" he asked.

"There's nothing there to find," I said.

"But that's what you took the SATs for. So you could go to college and—"

"That's just it, Dad. I didn't."

Seconds of silence. Tiny flickers of movement on my dad's face. "You didn't what?"

I told him then. How I ditched the SATs. How I killed two hours on a bus stop bench rather than go in and take the test.

Dad blinked furiously. "You kept this from me all week?"

"All week," I murmured softly.

"I asked, 'How'd it go?' "—Dad half rose from his seat—"You said, 'Fine.' *That was all a lie?*"

I nodded yes.

Dad pushed the chair back, stormed to the counter, wheeled around quickly. "How long before you were going to tell me the truth?"

Three, four years, I thought, but knew better than to say it.

Dad swallowed a couple times, hovering over me—and sat back down. "It's not too late," he said at last.

"I know. I heard there are SATs next month, I'll register on Monday—"

"No." I looked up, startled. He was pondering me, his chin resting on his fist. "I want you to take it, yes. But what I meant was—it's not too late to find there is something to Paulie Lockwood."

I snorted, "Yeah, right."

"You can start tomorrow. Start with the game."

"Forget about the game," my voice trembled, "and forget about me, okay?" I sniffed back tears. " 'Cause I have. Don't you get it, Dad? I don't even deserve to be on the team."

"Paulie. . . ."

"I *don't*." That spilled out, too, how Todd had blackmailed Benedict into keeping me.

Dad leaned forward. "Paulie. Did you ever think that when

Coach Z puts you out there in the sixth or seventh inning he must see something in you to do that?"

I dismissed it with a wave. "That's just because Bates is so bad in the field."

"What about the game this week, where you scored that run from third?"

"Big deal, there was a fly ball, I was on third. Anybody would have—"

"But didn't you tell me Coach Z had worked with you on tagging up?"

"Yeah, so?"

"And on Monday's game, where you slid into second and dodged the tag? He worked with you on that, too, right?"

"Those are all little things," I said. "Coach Z drums that stuff into me every day."

"See? He takes the time—"

" 'Cause he feels sorry for me. That's all it is."

"Then why does he put you in the game?"

"I don't know. He's a nice guy, he wants to give everybody a chance to play. . . ."

"In the late innings of a close game? He's that nice? Think, Paulie. He's putting you in because you *can* do those things."

"Wait a minute," I said. "How'd you know I scored from third that game?"

Dad's face went blank. "You told me."

"No, I didn't. And that other game, where I slid into second, I *know* I didn't tell you that."

"Well, uh—"

"You've been coming to the games, haven't you?" Dad's

cheeks colored. "You *have*. Even when I asked you not to. What'd you do, hide behind the backstop and *spy* on me?"

He shrugged, pleading innocence. "Can't I just come because I like baseball?"

"You don't like baseball *that* much. You're—why *did* you come?"

He looked at me. "Why do you think?"

"You came . . . because of me."

He nodded.

"So you came to all these games, hiding, just to see if I'd get up to bat, just to see me ground out—"

"Just to see you," Dad said.

"Man." I ran my hands through my hair. "Parents can sure be sneaky."

He laughed. "You know, your mom and Tyler and I were thinking we'd drive over to Hazelton to see you play tomorrow."

It didn't register at first, and then it hit me: Hazelton. The college stadium. The first sectional game with Westfield Tech. I heard my dad's words, *Just to see you*, echo in my head, and suddenly I wanted to play more than anything—just one inning, if that was all Coach put me in for, let me chase down a groundball, slap a hit to the opposite field. But even if I sat on the bench it would mean something. I wouldn't be there as anybody's favor. I'd be there as Paulie Roy Lockwood. All debts were canceled.

"You know," Dad said, "Todd going to Plattsburgh reminds me. I have to do some traveling this summer, out to Rochester, Buffalo, and I thought . . ."

I eyed him warily.

"I thought maybe you'd want to come along, just you and me, and—well, maybe check out some of the colleges, up in that area."

He was good, all right. Casual, as if the idea had just occurred to him.

"Aww. . . ." I felt my whole body retract. "I don't think so. . . ."

"On the way back," he said, "we could stop by Cooperstown."

My mouth went dry. "Cooperstown?"

"We wouldn't be far from it. Isn't that where the Hall of Fame is?"

"*Of course* that's where the Hall of Fame is," I said. "You know perfectly well that's where—"

"So do you want to go?"

"You know what this is?" I tried to look aloof, but my grin broke through. "This is a bribe."

"Well, you know," Dad said, "parents can sure be sneaky."

I lay in bed, the house so silent I could hear every spring in my mattress. And when it was obvious sleep wasn't coming any time soon, I leaned over to my nightstand and fiddled with the shortwave radio till I tuned in a game.

I recognized the announcer's voice immediately, and smiled. The Indians. They were still on the West Coast, at Oakland now. I shook my head. The road trip from hell; every time I had chanced upon their games they were losing. But I didn't care about the score—it was that announcer's voice I liked. A warm voice, and confident, painting a picture there on the field a guy could get so wrapped up in he didn't have to think of anything else.

One out in the top of the ninth, Indians down by five. I punched up my pillow and lay back. Oakland brought in some hot rookie reliever and he blew away the last two Indian batters on about eight pitches. I reached over lazily to turn the radio off, but waited until the announcer read the score one more time, and went through the totals. *"Game time four o'clock tomorrow afternoon, hope we see you then."* He said his name, and signed off.

Five minutes later I was still staring at the radio.

His name was Herb Score.

Chapter 22

"Tyler." I bumped over a stack of software boxes as I groped my way to his bed. "You awake?"

I shook his elbow and asked again. He stirred and sat up. "What's the matter?"

"You remember Herb Score?"

"*Who?*"

"I told you about him," I said. "He was a pitcher, and he lost an eye, and—come on, you remember."

"If you say so." He squinted at the clock beside his bed. "Paulie, it's the middle of the night."

"Well, listen," I said. "I just found out. He's a broadcaster for the Indians."

"So?"

"What I mean is—he didn't just *disappear.* He's still in baseball. He's an announcer. A *good* announcer."

"What's so special about that?"

"I told you, when he was young, he got hurt—"

"And?"

"Well . . . he went on."

"Of course he went on. What'd you think, his life just

stopped?" Tyler shook his head in bewilderment. "He had to do *something*, didn't he?"

"Yeah," I agreed. "He had to do something. He *had* to."

"So," Tyler grumbled. "Who else should we wake with the news?"

"Sorry," I muttered. "See you in the morning." I was halfway to the door, thinking I'd only confuse him if I said *There's somebody it woke up more than you.*

"Paulie, wait," he called. His voice was a lot less snotty. I lingered by the door. "Did Mom or Dad tell you what happened?"

"Nobody told me anything," I said.

In the dim light, sitting up in bed in his pajamas, he looked about nine years old. He whispered, "You know how I wanted to get out of honors English?" I crept back to a chair. "And how you wouldn't even try to help me?"

"I remember," I nodded.

"So I did it myself. I got into the school system." He leaned forward, for a moment entranced in telling me. "I had the user ID, remember? And the SYSOP password?"

"Oh, of course." I rolled my eyes. "How could I forget?"

"So I figured, if I could get to the school records, get into the honors list, delete my name—"

"Wait—you broke into the school records? And you didn't think they'd notice?"

"I breached the system, got to the class rosters—and it froze on me." He hesitated. "Are you understanding this?"

"Not exactly."

"The damn thing *froze* on me. And there was a timer on it,

223

so they could tell who was using which terminal—do you understand *that?*"

I shook my head.

"They could tell this all happened at three-thirty from the computer room, and since I was the only one *in* the computer room then, the library aide remembered me. So—"

"So you got caught."

"Yeah."

"That I understand."

"Can you believe it?" he whined. "*One* kid does *one* crummy unauthorized class change in a school of *nine hundred,* and *still* he gets caught."

"Boy," I tried to keep my voice even, "computers are amazing, aren't they?"

"Maethner wants to ban me from the computer room for the rest of the year. And maybe next year, too. And Mom and Dad said fine." He mimicked them, " 'Tyler's got to learn to take his medicine.' "

I reached out and patted his shoulder. "It'll be okay," I said, rising and heading for the door. "Listen, I've got to get some sleep. I've got a big game tomorrow."

"Paulie," he whispered. I turned. "I was wondering . . ." His voice lifted with hope. "You think they might throw me out of the honors program for this?"

"I don't know. Maybe." I smiled in the darkness. "If you're lucky."

I didn't really have a chance at sleep, though I gave it a shot. When I heard the *thump* of the newspaper landing on the front porch I considered it officially morning, and raced down-stairs.

That was when I thought about Melissa.

I thought of how many times I'd been a jerk around her, cut her off, walked away in midsentence, turned in probably the worst garbage on paper the world had ever seen, and she smiled and took a deep breath, showed me how to make it better, and printed it.

I waited until eight-thirty, and then I left for her house. Soon I was trotting, and by the time I rang her bell I had soaked my shirt through in the warm morning sun.

Her mother answered the door and let me in. She glanced quickly at the big damp spots on my T-shirt, the limp strands of hair creeping under my Cardinals cap, but all she said was, "Well, you must be thirsty." She stuck a big glass of orange juice in my hand, and called up to Melissa's room.

Halfway down the stairs Melissa saw me, and stopped.

"Hi," I said.

"What do you want?" She marched right past me out to the porch. At the far end there was an old swing. She climbed in, tucked her legs up, clasped the chain, and stared straight ahead.

I took a few steps closer. "Remember yesterday, when you came up to my room?" About as delicately as I could I sat at the other side of the swing.

"Yes," Melissa said. "I remember it very well."

"Remember how you were going to tell me . . . what you thought of me?" She almost turned at that. I kept on. "And I didn't let you. I took everything you said and twisted it around."

"You did." She still hadn't looked over, but I could tell, I had her interested.

"And . . . well, I'm sorry, Melissa." My voice was raspy. "With Todd, this whole year—I didn't know what to do, and there were times I needed somebody—and that was you."

She drew her knees up to just below her chin. Out of the corner of her eye she watched me.

"You didn't owe me anything—you didn't owe *Todd* anything. But I always acted as if you did. Because, I guess, I thought that I did."

"If I was any help," she said quietly, "it was because I wanted to be."

"So, I—" I looked at my sneakers, then leaned in front of her so she had to see me. "Well, I want to know."

Her eyebrows rose. "Know what?"

"What you think of me," I said. "I'd like to know."

She waited just a couple of seconds. Finally she reached out. I thought at first she was going to punch me on the shoulder the way she always did when she was teasing me. But her hand passed my shoulder, and for a moment touched my cheek. "I think you're my friend, Paulie. I'm happy you're my friend."

"Good." I blinked. "That's what I want to be."

Melissa reached down and squeezed my hand, while the swing swayed in the faint breeze.

"You know," I cleared my throat, "for a moment, when you and Todd were together in my room yesterday, I thought—I wondered if . . ."

Melissa stretched out a toe and pushed off from the railing

so that the swing began to rock. "If we could still be Todd and Melissa again, right?"

"That's right."

She looked off. "There are times I wish Todd and I were still together. I think about things we did."

"In your car," I said. "Going cruising in your car."

"That was fun." Her face brightened. "And you in the back-seat, always bitching about my driving—"

"And you and Todd, fighting over the radio—"

"And you saying some pitcher I never heard of had the *best change-up in the major leagues*—"

"And you saying, 'What's a change-up?' "

"And you just about wedged between the seats, up in front with us."

"And then at that certain hour, you always had to get rid of me—"

"We didn't—"

" '*Where should we let you off, Paulie?*' "

"Well, you could never take a *hint*—"

Melissa went red and we both broke up, giggling. When we caught our breath she said softly, "We're still all friends. There's no reason why we couldn't do something like that still. . . ."

I started to agree, but my throat felt tight and the words got lost.

With both hands she clasped the chain and leaned her cheek against her wrists. "I guess some things just aren't meant to be."

The two of us rocked gently at opposite ends of the swing. "No," I said hoarsely, watching her. "No, they aren't."

Melissa's mother poked her head out the door to ask if we wanted some breakfast.

"I almost forgot," I said. "You'd better give me that thing you wanted to give me in the library."

"The recorder," she said.

"Yeah. That's it."

"But—why do you want—"

"For the *game*, Melissa. Sheesh." I shook my head in exaggerated wonder as her eyes grew large.

"You're going to cover the game!" She grabbed my arms and shook me. "Paulie, that's great."

"Yeah, yeah," I said, blushing. "Well, just give it to me, will you? After all," I winked, "we've got a newspaper to get out."

Chapter 23

He was late. Or maybe I was early. Or maybe he had gone a different way, or gotten a ride, and meeting me on the corner, the same corner where we'd met to walk to school for eight or nine years now, hadn't even crossed his mind. So finally I gave up on glancing at my watch and waiting, and I hurried on. When I saw him at school as the team was climbing on the bus for the ride to Hazelton I never even asked him how he got there.

I hardly asked him anything. He just nodded coolly, and I nodded back, and when I saw an empty seat next to Luther Henderson I took it, and he settled for a seat up front. The rest of the guys were getting all psyched for the game, hooting how they were going to pound Westfield Tech. I kept my eyes away from Todd and dug Melissa's recorder out of my duffel bag. Coach Z was trying to take attendance and yelling to keep the noise down. "Where's Spiros?" Austin Wolfe wondered, and Emo said he had to play some con-*sert*-o today, and Frankie Flynn said, "Duh, Emo, it's con-*chair*-toh." With the two of them hollering back and forth and other guys joining in we were like a kindergarten class on its first field trip.

What was I waiting for? I clicked on the recorder. "Edgeview versus Westfield Tech, May twentieth," I crooned in a reporter's tone. Then I made a big show of striding down the aisle, right past Todd, down to where Harley Shawn was sitting.

"Harley," I said loudly into the recorder, "this is the biggest game of your high school career. . . ."

But it wasn't just the journalist in me speaking, I knew then. It was to spite Todd, to make sure he knew I was somebody, too. When the story came out in *Panther Paws* it'd be my name everybody would see under the headline—my name, and nothing to do with him.

"Tell us," I said to Harley, making certain Todd could hear, "how do you stand up to the pressure?" But when I stuck the recorder in front of Harley's face he just scowled at me from beneath the brim of his cap and reeled off a string of curses.

"No, really," I tried, "what do you think the key is—"

By now everybody had seen the recorder, and guys were leaving their seats to speak into it, trying to be funny. *"Everybody sit down,"* Coach Z hollered. I retreated to my seat.

"You could tell the team was ready," I said into the recorder. "The players were loose. . . ."

They were even looser when Ozzie Fuentes clubbed a bases-loaded double in the third to put us up by three. With our first few hits I had leaped off my seat with the others to cheer, once banging my head on the ceiling of the dugout. After that I tried to stay calm, but how could I? Just being in the locker room before the game was a thrill, with the carpeted floor, and the showers.

"This is like the Big Time," Tommy Ricco yelled as we suited up.

230

"Where's my sneaker deal?" Emo giggled. "Where's my agent?"

I flinched a little when I heard that, but when I glanced at Todd across the room he didn't seem bothered; he was just pulling on his jersey with a thin smile. Okay, to hell with him, I thought, as we filed through the tunnel out to the dugout. He sat at the far end, wedged between the wall and Coach Z. To hell with him; he doesn't need *anybody*.

Harley had his stuff today: he struck out a couple in the first, and a couple in the second. By the top of the fourth he was starting to strut the way he always did when things were going well, pumping his fist on a strikeout, turning his back on a pop-up before the ball was even caught. He wasn't always getting strikes with his pitches on the corner, but that seemed to make him cockier still. Once, after the ump called a ball, Harley retreated to the far side of the mound, shaking his head so everyone could see how disgusted he was before he stepped to the rubber again for his sign.

We added two more runs in the fourth on a double by Tommy Ricco. In the top of the fifth I winced when Steve Bates played a ground ball as if he were a World Cup soccer star, booting it once, twice, three times. A couple of batters later he threw a double-play ball into left field for Westfield's first run. So it was 5–1 by the top of the sixth. You could tell Harley was tiring a little. His fastball was sailing out of the strike zone. When he walked the leadoff batter that inning he just grunted. When he walked the second guy we could hear him grumble. He got a pop-up for the first out, but up next was their big cleanup hitter, Pollack—the same guy who had homered off

Harley a month ago and then charged the mound. In the second inning Harley had whiffed him on an off-speed curve. But this time, when he missed high for ball three, Harley shot the ump an ugly glare.

"Bear down, now," Coach Z yelled. "Throw strikes."

He did, but Pollack jumped on a fastball down the middle and lined a single to left, scoring their second run.

Even over the roar of the Westfield crowd I could hear Harley curse. He didn't even concentrate on the next batter, walking him on five pitches, and that just set him off more. With the bases loaded he barely took the time to get Emo's sign before flinging a pitch in to the new hitter, a lefty, who pulled a low line drive toward first. Luther Henderson went down like a hockey goalie to stop it. The ball ricocheted off his glove and lay spinning a couple of yards away. Luther scooped it up, tagged the base, then threw to Austin Wolfe covering second for the tag on Pollack, and we were out of the inning.

While our guys were going three up, three down in the bottom of the sixth, Harley stalked from one end of the dugout to the other like a cooped-up leopard at the zoo. When Luther took a pitch in the dirt, he yelled, "Oh, call it a strike, call it a strike." Out of Coach Z's earshot he cursed the ump, then their big hitter Pollack, then the Westfield fans, then the ump again.

When Luther flied out to end the inning, Coach Z laid his hand on my shoulder and I nearly jumped.

"Paulie," he said. "You're in for Bates. I need your defense out there; play second."

I tried to swallow; it felt like a bird's nest going down. Then

I couldn't find my glove (I was *holding* it all along). The other guys were already out at their positions, and from everywhere I heard stamping, whistling, shouting for the last three outs. I staggered to the top step of the dugout and then hesitated, as if I wanted to give Coach a chance to change his mind.

That was when I saw Todd. For the first time all day he didn't duck my glance. He nodded, and made fists of both hands to hearten me.

I turned away without acknowledging.

"Paulie, *let's go.*" Coach Z clapped his hands.

I ran out to second. Harley was wrapped so tightly on the mound he didn't even notice me. When he walked the first batter on four straight I called, "Bear down, Harley, nothing to worry about." But I wasn't so sure. I could see his pitches now a lot better than I could from the dugout. His fastball was drifting high and the curve had flattened out.

The Westfield runner edged off first. I crouched, ready. The next batter topped a slow roller out toward Austin Wolfe at short. I raced over to cover second, but Austin's only play was at first.

With one out we loosened up and got a little louder, talking it up behind Harley. But nobody was louder than he was. When he missed his next two pitches low he rang off a curse with each one. The ump stepped around in front of Emo, shot Harley a glance, and pretended to sweep off the plate, but the message was clear—watch your mouth. Then Harley got that hitter on a pop-up to Frankie Flynn. Two outs. One more and he could swear all he wanted to in the locker room.

Harley dug at the rubber while the Westfield runner inched carefully off second. He tried a slow curve that broke only letter high, and the ump called it a ball.

"Bad call," Harley muttered, *"bad call,"* snapping his glove at Emo's return throw and storming once around the mound.

"Play ball," the ump called out to him. "Take a walk later."

But all Harley heard was *walk.* "What?" he yelled back to the ump. "What'd you say to me?"

"Hey, Harley," I cautioned, and Austin Wolfe and I trotted toward him. "What he meant was . . ." But Harley glared us both back to our positions.

"Let's go, Harley," Coach Z called from the dugout. "Throw strikes." It was just what he always said. But this time Harley took it personally and for a moment even flashed the coach a dirty look.

I read Emo's sign—fastball—and cheated a step to my left. Harley reared back and tried to gun it in so hard the ball bounced a foot before the plate. Emo made a nice stop and the runner held. The next pitch was wild high. Then, after staying in his stretch for what seemed like half a minute, Harley aimed a slider right over the plate.

It broke just low. "Ball four," the ump called.

Harley went berserk. "Ball four?" He took a couple steps toward the plate. "How was that ball *four?*"

"Settle down, son," the ump said patiently.

That only made it worse. "Settle down?" Harley barked. By now our side of the crowd was booing the ump and the Westfield side was booing Harley. I saw Coach Z climb out of the dugout and jog toward the mound. "Maybe," Harley raged, "if

234

I got a goddamn *strike* call now and then I *would* settle down."
Coach Z laid a hand on Harley's shoulder but he ripped free.
"Maybe if I wasn't getting *squeezed* on *every single pitch*—"

The ump pulled off his mask and marched toward Harley.
"Are you questioning my ball and strike calls?"

Coach Z looped an arm around Harley's middle, and
Luther Henderson had hold of his left arm. Too bad nobody
covered his mouth. "No, *duh*," Harley snorted, spit flying, "I'm
questioning your taste in *ties*. What do you *think* I'm—"

In one perfect pivot the ump turned and flung his right
arm toward the stands. *"You're out of this game."*

A half second later a raucous cheer went up from the Westfield fans. Harley's face blanched. When Luther, in surprise, let
go of him, he almost crumpled to the ground. "I'm *what?*" He
turned to us, his whole body swaying. *"What'd* he say?"

The ump was explaining to Coach Z, "I'm just going by
the rules. Your boy"—he motioned to Harley, whose mouth
now was twitching as if he would cry—"just wouldn't let it go."

Coach Z's voice was hoarse. "That's all right, that's the rule."
It was Harley he was angry with. He shoved him toward the
dugout. "Go sit in the locker room." We watched Harley trudge
off like a kid being sent to bed without supper while the Westfield stands rocked with jeers.

The ump flipped open a notepad from his back pocket.
"Coach, who you bringing in?"

"Yeah," Frankie Flynn mumbled beside me. "Who we
bringing in?"

"I guess Spiros—" I began, then remembered he was gone.
Luther said, "Gotta be"—his voice died as he turned and

saw Bates on the bench, out of the game. He shook his head. "Can't be," he mumbled.

Coach Z took a sideways glance at the dugout.

The ump waited. "Coach?"

"Number twenty-seven," Coach Z said faintly. "Bannister." He cupped his hands, and his scratchy voice pierced the crowd noise as he called Todd to the mound.

Todd bounded up immediately, grabbing his glove without the least sign of nerves.

I was the one whose legs went silly.

"Coach," I said. "You can't . . ."

"I have to, Paulie." He rubbed up the ball, and lifted his eyes to mine. "Who else we gonna use?"

"You're going to put him in right here," I said. "In *this* spot?"

"All we need," he muttered stubbornly, "is one more out."

"But, Coach," I said. "Todd can't do it."

I never got to hear his answer. The Edgeview crowd was coming out of its shock over Harley getting tossed. When they saw Todd loping to the mound, adjusting his goggles with his glove tucked under his arm, they were thrown again. And then they got loud. By the time Todd joined us on the mound the cheers were resounding through the stadium.

"Take all the time you need, son," the ump said. Todd and I exchanged a quick, shy look. Coach Z started talking about the next batter, but I could tell by his tone what he was really saying was *I'm sorry to do this to you, son.* Todd just nodded and took the ball. The rest of the infielders patted his back, called,

"You're the man, Todd." "One out, baby, just one more out." After several warm-up pitches I was still standing there, alone at the edge of the mound. My own words, *Todd can't do it*, kept ringing through my head.

Todd took a throw back from Emo and turned to me. I started back to second. "Paulie, wait," he called. "You scared?"

I nodded. "A little, yeah."

"Hey, what do you know?" He loosed a nervous grin. "Me, too."

The ump hollered, "Play ball." Todd's first pitch was a strike on the inside corner. The Edgeview crowd went nuts. I feinted toward second to keep the lead runner close. Then Todd tried a slow curve, but it didn't break. The batter staggered backward to avoid getting hit.

"Now, throw it now," I muttered to myself. That old fastball. Just once, reach down and hum it past this guy, just once.

He threw a fastball then, but it was nothing special, and the batter was ready. He drove a sharp single to left center. The runner on second scored and made it 5–3. The cheers of the Westfield crowd seemed to reach me through a long tunnel.

Still runners on first and second, still two outs. Todd missed with another mediocre fastball outside. I felt my whole body slump. What was I hoping for, that suddenly he would turn on the heater and have perfect control? That it would be like it used to be, if only for one out?

No, I knew better. I took a peek at their on-deck circle. The big guy, Pollack, glowered like a pro wrestler.

Todd went to the curve again, but it looped in at shoulder

level for a ball. The batter dug in eagerly now with the count two-and-oh. I couldn't hear a sound from our side of the stands.

He missed with another fastball outside. Then for just a second he glanced over at me. I raised my eyebrows as if to say *What is it?* but he looked back in for Emo's sign. I knew he wouldn't try the curve again—and so did the batter. He counted on that nothing fastball, and when he got one, roped a liner between short and third.

Tommy was playing too deep in left to have any chance at nailing the baserunner, so I took his throw at second. I saw guys in the Westfield dugout laughing, and wearing rally caps, and why not? They were just one run down now, 5–4, had men on first and third, and their cleanup hitter, Pollack, was nearing the plate, the bat like a breadstick in his big hands.

Todd looked to both sides to check the runners. Then he stepped off the rubber to turn and see where the outfielders were positioned. He leaned in for the sign. Stepped off the rubber again to grab the resin bag.

"Come on," I mumbled, and slapped my glove in despair. "Just get it over with."

Pollack waggled his bat through the strike zone, waiting.

Todd stepped off the rubber again. Over on the Westfield side they started booing. When I looked up, Todd was signaling me toward him with his glove.

I trotted over. "Can you still throw that pitch?" he asked. "That stupid pitch of yours, what'd you call it?"

I had to stop and think, and then choked out, "My knurve?"

"Yeah." Todd licked his lips and eyed the dugout, where

238

Coach Z was standing on the top step watching us. "Well, can you throw it here?"

"Throw it?" I waited for his face to crack into a grin, but his stare through those goggles burned into me. "You're crazy," I said.

"Paulie, you've got to." Coach Z was hustling out toward us. The Westfield fans were catcalling, and the ump was ambling our way. "This guy'll kill my fastball. He's just waiting for it."

That fastball, sure, I thought.

Todd said, "But we can get him out with a breaking pitch. He's overeager, he'll swing too soon."

"So throw your curve," I barked.

"I *can't*," he shouted back. "You know that. I don't *have* a curve anymore. I can't get it near the plate."

I stammered, "I can't. . . ."

"I'll go play second."

"*You'll* play second?"

Emo arrived at the mound. "Wait a minute. You want *Lockwood* to pitch?"

"Just for this Pollack guy. If he gets a hit . . ." Todd shrugged. "Well, if he gets a hit, they get the lead. Maybe it's over. I'll come back and pitch till we get the third out."

I shook my head and tried again. "I can't believe . . ."

"He's a sucker for a breaking pitch," Todd pressed. "That's how Harley got him in the second. If you throw that knurveball of yours, we might have a chance. If I throw a fastball—it's over."

Coach Z scampered up the mound, more perplexed than mad, but mad was gaining. "What the hell's going on?"

Todd launched into his plan. Coach Z pulled back, frowned in disgust—but still listened.

More than I was, anyway. Instead I was muttering to myself, *I can't believe you're doing this to me.* Because that's what it was—Todd bailing out, here where it counted. And where was Paulie? Where he always was, tagging along, picking up after him. The gofer, the personal assistant. And this was the way he finished us, as if turning his back on me last night wasn't bad enough. This was the final go-screw-yourself. Hey, Paulie, mind throwing the pitch that ends the season? Mind letting me off the hook?

After all, what are friends for?

"Come on, Coach," Todd urged. "You're always saying we can't be afraid to try something different. So try this."

Coach Z shuffled his feet uncertainly. No way, I thought with relief. No way Coach Z was going to go for something crazy like this. Todd didn't understand. Coach only *talked* about those daring moves. Deep down he was the guy who did just what Maethner ordered, played it safe.

Then Coach Z gestured to the ump for another few seconds and turned to me. "What about it, Paulie?" He wrung his cap in his hand. "You want to give it a shot?"

My eyes grew wide. I turned on Todd. "You never noticed stuff like that before," I snapped, as if I could catch him in his scheme. "Who swings at what kinds of pitches. Who goes for *breaking balls.* Since when do you know about that?"

"What do you think I've been doing, sitting on the bench all season," he said. "Feeling sorry for myself?"

He was right, of course. Pollack was a sucker for a curve.

Todd didn't have a curve anymore. I had . . . well, whatever I had, Todd thought it might work.

"Paulie, it's up to you," Coach Z said.

"Okay," I swallowed. "I'll try it."

I stepped to the rubber and Todd tossed me the ball. It felt huge, like a grapefruit in my hand. From far away the sounds of the stands reached me—some jeers from Westfield, and from our side, the murmur of confusion.

By now the Westfield coach was pointing to me and insisting to the ump, "He doesn't get any warm-ups, right?" The chance for an argument seemed to wake up Coach Z. He stuck his nose in there with them, yelled and gestured in every direction. Finally the ump stepped around him and said to me, "Play ball, son. No warm-ups."

I could tell our guys were in shock, seeing me up on the mound. Todd took my spot at second. Coach Z drifted hesitantly toward the dugout, shaking his head as if afraid to leave me there. I dug at the rubber with my right foot, trying to avoid so much as a peek at Pollack in the batter's box, and trained my eyes on Emo. By now our fans had caught on, and I felt it before I heard it—something swelling slowly from the stands. It rolled down onto the field like a gust of wind before a rain. I glanced up. They were standing now, and so were the Westfield fans, and for a second or two I let it all rush in, the cheering, the stamping of feet, a thousand faces all looking at me. And when it seemed they couldn't get louder, I checked the runner at third, reared back, and tried to burn a fastball right past Pollack.

The fastball Todd wouldn't throw, I did. Or thought I did.

For Pollack blinked eagerly when he saw it. His bat blurred through the strike zone, the metal *clanked* like a saw blade striking steel as he pummeled the ball in a huge arc to left. My head jerked around to follow its path. Tommy Ricco didn't move, just turned to watch it soar past. The roar of the Westfield fans felt like the sky tumbling down. Then, from the Edgeview kids, a colossal sigh of relief as I saw the ball hook into the stands, just left of the foul pole.

Too bad we didn't have an oxygen tank. In the time it took me to rub up a new ball, they could have wheeled it out to all the guys in the field and half the fans. I eyed Todd warily. He sent me a scolding stare, and his lips moved. I squinted to read them.

Who do you think you are? he said.

I stepped to the rubber. "Let's go, Paulie," Coach Z yelled from the dugout. The fans were still on their feet, the noise winding up again. Pollack hovered over the plate. I peered in at Emo. Frankie Flynn was hugging third, and Austin Wolfe was way over, too.

With the ball in the claw-handed grip of the knurve, I went into the windup. The runner at third took a few steps down the line. I kicked hard, as if I were coming in with another fastball, and snapped off the knurve as hard as I could, even if my wrist went with it.

Pollack swung; I heard a *ping,* another huge roar, and then my name, *Paulie, Paulie,* from all parts of the field.

There was the ball, bouncing slowly along the first-base side, halfway between the mound and the foul line. My God, it worked! I thought, as if that was all there was to it. But if I was slow to react, so was Pollack. He flung the bat away, lumbered out of the box like a locomotive mustering up speed.

"Take it," Emo yelled, straddling the plate as the runner from third raced home. "Go to first, go to first."

By now Pollack had huffed halfway to the bag. I scrambled awkwardly off the mound, scooped up the ball. Covering first, Luther held out his glove for a target. I drew my arm back—in my head I heard Coach Z's voice, *Bend your back, bend your back, bend your back*—and fired the ball to Luther, following through so the throw wouldn't sail. .

We nailed Pollack by a yard.

I never even saw the ump call him out, for Todd slammed me to the ground, trying for a bear hug. "You did it," he yelled, pulling me to my feet and shouting, "You know what that was? *You know what that was?*"

"What?" I shouted back, the grin splitting my face.

"*That was your first save.*" He laughed, hugging me, and by then the rest of the guys had reached us and I disappeared under a crowd of bodies. For a while after that we jumped around on the field as if we were state champs. "Calm down, now, calm down," Coach Z was saying, but the way he was beaming and slapping backs, you could tell he was pretty giddy, too.

Kids from the stands were running out on the field. I tried to find my folks and wave to them, but it was too crazy. I got swept through the tunnel to the locker room, where we whooped and laughed like maniacs.

Some of the guys were yelling, "Who's next, who do we play next?" and Steve Bates was pouring quarters into a vending machine, shaking up cans of Coke and spraying them around the room. Suddenly I remembered Melissa's recorder. I squeezed between Rishi and Emo and tore through my locker until I dug it out of a pocket. Cackling like a madman, I switched it on and turned to face the room. "This is Paulie Roy Lockwood, reporting," I said, and said it again, I liked the sound of it so much. "I'm here in the victorious locker room of the Edgeview Panthers. . . ."

What a story, I giggled, darting around for quotes. There was Harley's tantrum, Westfield's last-inning rally, Pollack's long drive gone foul, and most of all there was Todd, coming back to the mound and calling me in to pitch—the gutsiest move in the world. I could even imagine the lead. *Though he won't get credit for a single out, Todd Bannister led the Panthers to victory Saturday. . . .*

But where *was* Todd? I hadn't seen him, I realized, since he raced over from second after the final out. I checked all corners of the room, even climbed a chair to see better. It was really crowded now: a few reporters had surrounded Coach Z, and there was Maethner, trying to high-five Luther Henderson, and even some parents were filing in—but no Todd.

He wasn't in the showers, either. Still in my spikes, clutching the recorder, I clattered around in search of him. By then I had to duck out quickly to avoid getting interviewed myself. I fled up the tunnel, pausing where it opened into the dugout. It was quiet there, and maybe I could figure where he might have gone. . . .

That's when I saw him.

Standing on the mound. Still in his uniform, surrounded

by the empty stands, he stared down and kicked at the rubber absently, and then, as if he'd caught himself in a bad habit, he straightened up. He looked toward third, then to the outfield, then back to home. The late afternoon sun was pouring in from the stands overhead, so he must not have seen me in the corner of the dugout where I watched. But I could see him, his face, and in the sunlight I saw the glint of tears. Silent tears. He wasn't sobbing. He didn't even look upset.

He was saying good-bye.

I laid the recorder down on the bench. There were questions for my story I had to ask him—but I could ask him later. First I wanted to run out there, take him in a big hug, maybe butt my head against his and make him laugh, we could both laugh though our foreheads would be ringing for days. . . .

But a step or two from the field I stopped. *Go on,* I thought. *He needs you.* But instead I eased back into the tunnel, still watching him. He squared his shoulders, staring in at the plate. I knew then I wasn't going out there. He needed me, all right, but right now he needed this. To stand by himself one last time until, nodding his head as if answering some voice inside, he walked off the mound and never once looked back.